Flaming Retribution

LAURA HAWKS

Copyright © 2016 Laura Hawks

Cover: Shutter Stock and

Dominique Goodall of Priceless Editing

Editing by Enterprise Book Service

All rights reserved.

ISBN-13: 978-0-9976594-1-2

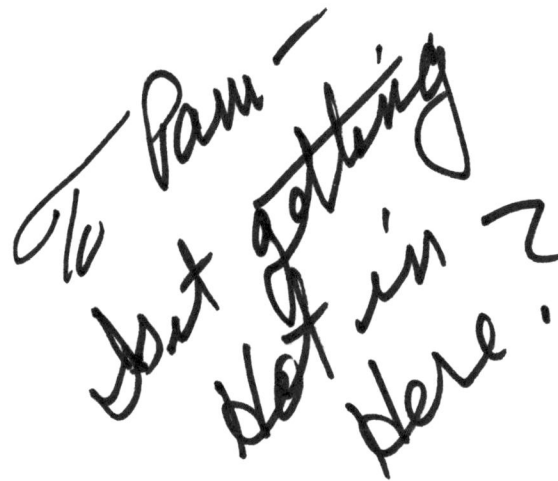

DEDICATION

Always for my Mom

Who I miss very much.

And to my fans who

Always make me smile.

Tom –
Is anything
out of
place?

Enjoy
Longboune
♡

PROLOGUE

He couldn't be the hero when he needed to be, but he could be the hero now. He walked around checking everything to make sure it was all set, all right. He had to save the others. Even if they didn't want saving or know he was intervening in any way. They probably didn't even realize he was saving them. He was okay with that because a hero didn't need to be recognized, praised or even shown gratitude, as long as he accomplished what he intended.

He was on a mission now. One he should have been on a long time ago—but then, he didn't know. How could he have known or even dreamed such a thing could happen to him? He thought the whole world was utopian. His family was perfect and he became blind in his complacency, his happiness. He didn't see the tragedies about to befall them all. How could he? How does anyone suspect when their world will come crashing down?

How was he to know, in the blink of an eye, his reality would come to an end, or that he would be the catalyst to change the world for the better? No longer could he turn a blind eye to what he should've seen long ago. Although he couldn't protect what was stolen from him, he could prevent others from suffering his fate.

He had to go through agony to see the true path of his life's work. A direction now lay before him, and he only had to follow it. He answered the calling with a determination he hadn't given to anything before, but then, this was a far more important deed than any previous demand on his existence. Similar to the proverbial Phoenix, his world had to be obliterated before he could arise from the ashes to change what was left for the better.

As he walked around the room, he made sure everything was ready. Each piece of the puzzle was easy to find in a local hardware or drugstore. He made sure he bought it all in small increments and at various locations. He always paid in cash, always wore a baseball hat or a hoodie, and never, ever looked up. He wasn't stupid by a long shot. He knew he had to remain anonymous in order to fulfill the enormous task bequeathed him. He couldn't be stopped, but he also wouldn't take any chances unnecessarily.

All that remained for this particular venture was to set the cell phone's alarm. He had made everything else in his basement earlier and brought it with him. A small divided plastic container held the fine dust created from the shavings of sparklers, as well as a separate mixture comprised of ammonia, hydrogen peroxide, rubbing alcohol and battery acid. He placed the infused container atop some kegs of whiskey.

Once the timer deployed, it would spark off the powdered form of the sparklers, which would flare up the upper sparklers still on their sticks. This, in turn, would melt the plastic keeping each chemical separate, so they would mix together and create an explosion. The whiskey keg would blow, the alcohol would spread the fire and the building would be destroyed. In the destruction, the flames would cleanse, vindicate and purify. He would gain retribution for his hubris in once having a perfect life. Only now, he would attain a peace previously denied.

Timer set. Bomb set. Yes. It was ready. Five down. Hundreds more to go. One day he may even be rewarded for his diligence. For now, he took what he could from what he did. He couldn't be a hero when he needed to be, but he could be a hero now.

CHAPTER ONE

Kendall Roberts sat in the car and looked up at the building. The shining lights of the neon signs blinked on and off to attract those who might be passing by, trying to entice them into the establishment. Honestly, this wasn't her scene, but she admitted she was becoming desperate and her writing was getting stale. She needed inspiration, something that would get her creative juices flowing once again. Biting the bullet, she headed to the one place she thought for sure she would never visit. Desperation really did encourage people to do things they would never before consider, and she was definitely desperate.

Kendall couldn't help but contemplate what brought her to this point as she gathered up her courage to leave the vehicle and go inside the Cock-a-doodle Male Revue. Her life had been turned upside down months ago, and she would admit she was still trying to find her footing. It was difficult suddenly being alone. How ironic she never thought things like this would actually happen to her, or coming here would be something she finally resorted to.

Memories flooded her about her situation. Tears welled up in her eyes. Shit. She hated being so weak, feeling so vulnerable and seeming to cry at the drop of a hat. Angrily, she wiped her eyes and once again stared at the building.

A delivery truck caught her eye as it pulled past her to start unloading at the back door. Laughter then drew her attention to a couple of small groups of women headed towards the entrance. One was led by a woman wearing a sash that declared to the world she was turning 30. The other was led by a woman wearing a crown with an attached short veil and a t-shirt stating she was the bride, while her friends wore similar shirts that boldly declared them as bridesmaids. The building would definitely be packed, which was a blessing for Kendall, as she could remain in the back and hopefully be unobserved. The screaming women should draw all the attention away from her, and she was perfectly fine with that. This was, after all, a scouting and research mission. Nothing more. It wasn't a place for her to get cheap thrills or obtain some semblance of sexual excitement, unlike most of those who came, she assumed.

Realizing if she blended in with the two groups going in, no one else would realize she was alone. Kendall quickly hopped out of her car and jogged over. As suspected, the birthday group figured she was with the bridal group and the bridal group assumed the same in reverse. Trailing behind both, only the collector of admissions knew she was actually a party of one. When the hostess began to lead her to the front of the room, Kendall pulled her aside and asked to sit in the back.

"The view is much better in the front, dearie. You can see everything that way, and I do mean everything. I've a single still available." The scantily clad young hostess stated, surprised Kendall didn't jump at the chance to be in the first row of the show.

"No, thank you. I'm perfectly content to watch from the rear of the theater." Kendall lowered her voice conspiratorially. "I'll be able to see everything better all at once of what's occurring on stage from the back, more so than I can from the front."

The woman nodded. "Very true. Well the back isn't sold out, so sit anywhere there you'd like, but if you want anything from the bar, you'll have to get it yourself. The servers might not notice you sitting in the otherwise closed section. Enjoy the show."

Left to her own devices, Kendall chose a seat against the wall, yet still center stage. There were enough people in front of her she shouldn't even be noticed except by someone who was really looking. In addition, there was just enough dim light shining from the wall sconces that she could see to make notes, albeit with some difficulty. Once seated, she pulled out her pen and a small notepad. In truth, she would probably only watch closely and drink in all the information she could possibly use, making her notes at a later time. But just in case something in particular struck her, she could make a notation to be expanded upon without forgetting it.

The room filled up. Kendall felt like others were watching her, but the truth was no one was even paying attention to her. They were all in their own small groups, here to party and have fun, to drink and to get a bit wild. They were here to let loose and enjoy the eye candy that would be gyrating in front of them in a few more minutes. Not wanting to be solely the odd ball, she left her paper and pen on the table and headed to the little side bar to get a glass of wine. At least it might give her a focus, and maybe even steel her nerves so she stayed for the show instead of running out like the hounds of hell were at her heels. Truth was, if she did that, she would cause a bigger scene than she ever intended, and she was certainly not one to draw attention to herself.

Ironically, it was probably one of the reasons she was in this position to begin with. Kendall was an only child. She didn't know what it was like to have siblings to confide in, or fight with, or give her support when she needed it. Her father was a stern man, wanting to protect her from the harsh realities of the world.

Reg had joined the military, served in the Vietnam War, and acted like General Patton in keeping her safe. He would interrogate everyone who came to her house. He intimidated so many, she had only a very small handful of friends. She could never forget the time when she was in seventh grade and a boy who liked her walked her home, carrying her books. It was something she had always read about, but never thought happened in the current day and age.

When they arrived at her house, he handed Kendall her books. Reg met them on the porch and told her to go inside; he wanted to talk to the boy, whose name she no longer remembered. What she did recall, was after that talk, she never saw that boy again, not even in school. She always wondered what her dad said to him and where the boy went.

How did such a proud, strong, and some would

even describe him as hard, man commit suicide?

Kendall got her drink and returned to the table she had secured for herself just a short while earlier. Taking a sip of wine, she continued to wait for the show, her mind drifting back once again to her father.

She had just come home from work, her mother out, when she found her dad in his study. The back of the office chair faced her as she entered, his arm hanging limply from the side. She didn't think much of it, other than it was an odd position. When he didn't respond to her greeting, she walked around to the front of the chair only to find him slumped over, blood splattered over the back of the chair, a gun lying on the floor not too far from where his hand was draped over the arm. It took only a few milliseconds for the scene to register. Calmly, Kendall pulled out her cell phone and dialed 911. Then she called her mother and went to the living room to await the help she requested. She was never one to panic, always level headed and clear in what she needed to do in order to get something done. She assumed a large part of that was because of Reg and the military training that he passed on to her. He taught her to remain level headed; there would be time later and in private to break down, but first things first: do what needed to be done. So, that was what she did. She called for help and waited, trying to deal with the realization her dad was now gone and she would never again hear his laugh or feel his arms around her as he hugged her goodnight. That was over a decade ago and she still thought of him. She always would.

The lights dimmed further, then total darkness. A voice over the loudspeaker asked if everyone there was ready for the show, as well as a few dos and don'ts before the male performers took the stage. She pulled her cell phone over to be sure it was muted, then put it aside once again.

When the stage lights came up, there were seven men in an inverted 'V' formation, all dressed in nice looking business suits. Velcro suits. The men moved about the stage, dancing, swinging their hips, and pulling their clothes off with the distinct sound of Velcro pulling apart, heard over the loud, pulsating music. Kendall wondered if she actually heard it distinctly, or was it just her imagination because it was what she was expecting to hear? She wasn't sure what she was expecting, but the males moving out into the crowd was certainly not it. They would stand on the tables amid the women clamoring to touch them and stick dollar bills in their g-strings.

Kendall's eyes were on them, scanning, taking in as much as possible, but not for research. Instead, for pure interest, totally lost in the eye candy that was flagrantly displayed for her viewing pleasure as well as all the other women. Although they were all well built and good looking, they didn't seem to appeal to her as much as one in particular did. Maybe the others weren't her type or something, but the tallest one in the group with blondish hair took her breath away. It didn't help he seemed to be staring just as much at her. Their eyes continuously met and her heart began to beat wildly.

When they headed off the stage, Kendall let out

a breath she didn't even realize she had been holding. *Okay, that was useless. Get your head in the game, Kendall. You are here for a purpose. Focus!* She mentally berated herself.

Darkness descended again. The women were screaming in anticipation and excitement as one of the males took to the stage then hopped down to dance among the women. Kendall watched, taking note of his muscle movements. He picked the bride-to-be from the crowd of hooting and hollering females and brought her up on stage to sit in a chair put there by a stagehand. He danced for her, gyrating and taking her hand to move it along his chest down to just below the rim of his speedo underwear concealing his private parts. She blushed, laughed and grabbed for more. He pushed her legs open, kneeling in front of her.

Kendall's eyes were glued. She waited to see what would happen next, but at the same time, she was impressed with the male as it seemed as if all the other women in the room didn't exist to him. His focus was solely on the woman he was dancing for. Kendall's heart couldn't help but speed up as she watched, almost feeling as if she were a voyeur to something that should have been done privately. No, she wasn't a prude. She wouldn't be here if she were. She just felt like she was intruding with something that should have been more clandestine. When the dance was over, he led her down the stairs before he proceeded to exit the stage.

The show was mostly the same: the guys bringing to the stage their victims, arranging them in one position or another. This was what Kendall was here for. How long had it been since she had been with a man? To feel his body hovering over hers? She needed to see his muscles bunching, flexing, then relaxing as they moved as if they were making love to the fully clothed women they chose to dance for.

Kendall had finished her wine, her mouth dry from watching these men entertain the women before them. They seemed happy to be giving themselves to these women in such a display of flesh, leaving only minute details to the imagination.

Her eyes turned away for a moment, looking sadly at the now empty glass once filled with wine. When she turned back, he was in front of her, holding out his hand.

"Come with me," he demanded more than requested as he waited for her to take his extended offering.

She recoiled horrifically. "No. I… No."

He took a step closer, leaning down so there would be no mistaking his words against her ear. "Come with me. How would it look if I have purposefully come over here, to leave without you? Surely, you wouldn't wish to embarrass either of us at this point."

Peering around his good-sized frame, she could see the attention of the others were on them. The realization couldn't have made her any redder with embarrassment than she was already. Tentatively, slipping her hand in his, she stood. He pulled her on stage, giving her time to assess how gorgeous he was. He had dirty blond, wavy hair in a becoming style. His jaw line was angular, sharp, and wholly masculine. His eyes were a rich turquoise-blue and she wasn't sure if they were contacts or really that color. He had a bit of a five o'clock shadow, all the rage lately, giving him an unmistakable rugged appearance. He was taller than her. She would guess he was six foot two.

Compared to her smaller five foot eight, he towered above her. It was readily apparent he worked out. His shoulders were broad, his waist narrow, in that male-perfect way. He certainly had an eight pack with his abs, and the muscles in his arms definitely indicated he lifted weights. She had a feeling he could lift her easily, and she was not a small woman.

He indicated for her to sit on some spongy cushions already placed on the stage. Then, he started to dance and remove his clothes. She tried not to look, she tried to disappear from the others who were watching, but she knew she was unsuccessful. He was hypnotizing, and she couldn't resist staring as he moved with a surprising gracefulness around her. Soon, all but a g-string remained; he straddled her seated form, thrusting himself towards her body. He took her hands and placed them on his buttocks.

She could feel his ass muscles flex and tighten before he released them with his constant movements. She could see droplets of sweat and smell his masculine scent from his body as he danced extremely close. Even his manly scent was intoxicating, and for a brief instant she almost forgot where she was as she wanted to reach out with her tongue and run it against his tawny skin, which he displayed so prominently in front of her.

In just one instant the world melted away and she wanted to give in to her primal urges and desires. In the next moment, the song ended and he was moving one hand around to help her up from the cushions to lead her off the stage. He leaned over as the stairs loomed in front of her and softly whispered, "Hang around after the show?" He then kissed her cheek as she ambled, slightly dazed, back to her seat.

Definitely not, Kendall thought and rushed back to her seat as quickly as her feet could carry her. She was surprised and admittedly grateful to find another glass of wine where the empty goblet once stood. Without thinking, she picked it up and downed the whole thing in five large gulps. She was definitely a light weight when it came to alcohol. Within just a couple of minutes, she felt it slam against her head. The few things she was looking at wavered and seemed to be a bit off kilter as her vision blurred.

After the number where she was on stage, the whole group of dancers did a finale where they all came out for one additional set. She watched, note taking or anything else completely forgotten. Her cheeks felt intensely hot and she could only imagine how deep a red they were from the combination of the alcohol and embarrassment. The other women were too busy paying attention to the males on stage. They didn't give her a second thought, yet Kendall felt as if they were all looking at her, staring at her and judging her.

Chapter Two

Kendall was so lost in her own thoughts, as well as the fogginess created by the second beverage, she hadn't realized the show was over. The women were starting to depart the property almost in a rush, as if to get home and be with their partners after getting all worked up. She wanted to hide until they were all gone. She desired to be able to slither away unnoticed. As she started to stand, the room wavered in a spinning and distinctly unpleasant motion. She plopped back down to her seat and shut her eyes for a few moments in order to regain her equilibrium.

After what she thought was only a few moments, she realized the lights had gone out and there was a slight clinking of glasses by the bar as the bartender went about cleaning up. The crowds of exuberant women had died down a little bit ago, and she eventually realized they had all left. Opening her eyes, she almost jumped as she realized he was in front of her again.

"Thanks for waiting. I'm Skye Falcon." He held out his hand to her to shake hers, but she stared at it as if she had never seen a hand before. Frowning, Skye retracted his hand and motioned to the chair in front of her. "Mind if I join you?"

Dumbly, she shook her head. Was this really happening? He was…well, gorgeous. Just looking at him made her mouth feel as if she tried to drink a glass of sand; it was so dry. Between him and the second glass of hastily drunk wine, her senses were dulled and her head swimming.

"Are you okay?" he asked as he sat down. He knew he had an effect on women, but this one was starting to make *him* a bit nervous.

He couldn't help but spot her from the stage, despite her trying to almost blend into the background. She was very pretty with long, ebony hair and hazel-green eyes. Her skin was light, but she had a few freckles scattered about, giving her an innocent quality that he truly admired. It was plainly obvious she was by herself, and it was also pretty blatant she wasn't sure she wanted to even be here. That, alone, rather amazed him and made him seek her out.

So often the women here were looking for a quick feel, or a chance to have a bit of harmless fun before they went home to whatever man was waiting for them. In a way, Skye envied those other at-home men for they would get the wild, uninhibited women he just sent back to them. They would reap the benefits of their having sex in all the wonderful positions he and the other dancers demonstrated on stage. Most of the time, he was perfectly fine with that. He was here to entertain and open the minds of women to something more than the drudgery of their existences. He hoped to give them a few minutes of heaven using just their imaginations for the possibilities of what could be. Yet, at the end of the night, he went to his apartment alone. Except tonight. Tonight, Skye wanted company. Or more precisely, he wanted this intriguing young woman's company.

He didn't know why he found her so

interesting. Maybe because she was alone, although he had to admit he had seen several women in the club by themselves before. Housewives who wanted to escape without their husbands knowing where they were, or young women who wanted the chance to have a bit of fun and found no one to come with them, or even those who didn't want friends and family aware they went to a male strip club. She obviously wasn't one of the aforementioned ladies. She was timid, but she also seemed to have a purpose in being there. He had seen her writing on occasion, albeit he couldn't imagine someone writing a letter while in attendance to such an establishment. She piqued his curiosity and, for him, that was a rare occurrence indeed.

"Yes. I'm sorry. I had a second glass of wine and I guess I drank it too fast. It went right to my head."

"That can happen." He leaned forward, his elbows resting on the table between them. "Are you at least going to tell me your name?"

She blushed and looked away. He was really

too good looking to continually stare at. "Sorry. It's Kendall. Kendall Roberts."

"Nice to meet you, Kendall. I didn't mean to embarrass you earlier, but I must admit you caught my eye. You weren't here for the show, so I'm curious as to why you came."

Her eyes moved up to him in surprise. "How do you know I wasn't here for the show?"

"Because you hid in the back, you didn't look like you were having fun, and you didn't want to come up on stage. You also weren't here for the drinks, as far as I can discern, you only had two. So, again, why did you come if not for the eye candy and cheap thrills?"

She looked away embarrassed. *Oh yeah. Came to see how men moved as they made love so I could be more realistic when I wrote the sex scenes in my book. Why not from experience, you ask? 'Cause who the hell wants to make love to me? For that matter, why would I want to make love to most of the cretins who appear even partially interested? Of course, that's just what the most handsome guy I ever talked to wants to hear*, she admonished herself silently. Knowing he was waiting for an answer, she shrugged her shoulders. "Research."

"Dancer? Looking to steal some of our moves?" His sexy tone held a teasing quality.

"God, no," she laughed lightly.

He was surprised; her laughter reminded him of a soft, tinkering bell. "Then what are you researching?"

"Men's movements. How your muscles bunch and relax, how a body moves around so fluidly." Why in god's name was she even telling him this? For that matter, why was she even still sitting here when she should've left before he even came out?

More lights clicked off, leaving them in almost total darkness, save for a couple of nightlights on the wall sconces. He stood and waited for her. "We should go or we'll be locked up all night. Not that I would particularly mind."

Kendall blinked at his insinuation. She was sure booze and darkness would make it tolerable for a man like him to be with someone like her. She grabbed her writing journal, made her way towards the illuminated exit sign and out the door into the foyer, which would lead her outside to her vehicle. Although her head was still giving her wavering vision, it wasn't enough to prevent her from mostly walking straight.

"I'm still curious as to why you need to see body motions. Are you a physical therapist? A massage specialist? What are you doing with this information?"

"Writing. Sorry. I guess I should've mentioned it sooner. I write romance novels and I wanted to give them a bit more substance with descriptions of the way people move. This seemed like a good opportunity."

"Ah. That makes sense, though you might want to just install a few mirrors around your bedroom and watch whoever is with you in them. That might help too."

"Yes. I probably could do that," she admitted warily. If it were that easy to find someone she wanted to be intimate with just for research, she wouldn't have come to such a place as this to begin with.

Her hesitated response shocked him. "Don't you have someone to give you personal attention? Someone who could help you with your research?" Skye's eyes glanced appreciatively over her body once again, taking in her figure. She wasn't model thin, but he was personally fine with that. She wasn't overly obese, either. She was rather pretty, in a subdued way, but looks were never what meant anything to him. He was more into character and sense of being. He appreciated the fact she was uncomfortable and shy, maybe even a bit nervous. She still held her head high and took the challenge to get whatever she needed to do, done. There was an interior strength to her, which he admired, as well as a sweetness to her. She seemed like someone who would do anything for anyone, and to him that was a rare, unselfish quality he didn't get to see too often.

"Not really."

"Then I am very lucky you decided to come

here so I could meet you."

Kendall did something she didn't remember doing in a very long time. She actually blushed and was very grateful for the cover of darkness, disrupted only by a handful of dull parking lot lights.

Her attention was drawn away from him for a brief moment when she heard a vehicle speed away. *Drunken ass*, she thought before shaking her head and turning back to Skye. Honestly, it had been a very long time since she found herself in a position to flirt. She wasn't sure she remembered how, and she wasn't sure she wanted to. Why start something she was not going to be able to see through, or that was a joke to him? She knew she wasn't pretty enough for the likes of him. She wasn't thin enough for someone who had such a perfect body. The idea of harmless flirting, or anything else with this man, only made her feel more isolated and lonely. She didn't want a one night stand or to be another notch on his bedpost, and she sure as hell didn't want pity sex. She would rather go home and take care of any urges she had by herself than to be humiliated or worse, forgotten moments later.

"Yes. Well. Thank you for the dance. I should be going."

Skye seemed to instantly know his compliment derailed her. Suddenly, she couldn't seem to get away from him fast enough. It surprised him. She almost seemed appalled to be with him. Women were usually fawning over him, thrilled to have captured his attention and the possibility of being with him intimately, and yet, Kendall seemed to just want to run in the opposite direction as fast as she could. Maybe she only enjoyed women? To him, that was the only thing that made perfect sense. Kendall was not into men.

"You're welcome."

Kendall turned and headed towards one of only a few cars left in the parking lot. She could feel Skye's eyes on her, but just to be sure, she turned around to glance back at him and, sure enough, he was watching her. Giving a soft sigh, she turned away from him. *If only*, she thought. *If only I was thinner, prettier, more assured of my sexual aptitude. If only I didn't mind being a one night stand or having sexual relations just for the fun of it. 'Cause, damn. I have a feeling he would be really fun. But then what? I would just be lonely again. Clinging onto the memory of a great night, and somehow I know that would only make the following days all that much harder.*

She had almost reached her automobile when again a squealing car caught her attention. She hadn't even fully comprehended that this time the vehicle was swerving towards her. Within milliseconds of being crushed by the speeding car, she was thrown to the ground, a heavy weight on top of her. Rubber tires sprayed gravel up as the car pivoted about to again head towards the stunned couple. Skye rolled off of Kendall, grabbing her upper arm as he jumped up, pulling her along with him. He knew they had to get out of the area quickly if they were going to survive this maniac.

Chapter Three

Skye pulled her to a run, heading for a gate he knew the automobile couldn't fit through. He was also aware if the car didn't care about damage, it could plow through the fence and continue after them. He wasn't sure what was going on, but he didn't have time to think about it, either. Survival instincts kicked in. Live the next few minutes and figure out everything when they could breathe safely again.

He pushed her towards his shiny black GMC Sierra 1500 Denali. Lifting his wrist as he ran, he spoke into his watch. "Unlock. Start. Get in Kendall."

Skye ran around to the driver's side of the vehicle just as the car came crashing through the fence. He put the gear in drive as soon as Kendall climbed into the cab of the truck. He didn't wait. Once he saw she was in and started to pull the door shut, he stepped on the gas, bolting out of the parking lot like a bat out of hell with the car chasing after him. As he looked in the rearview mirror, a loud pop occurred, forcing even the heavy duty truck to bounce at the impact. Kendall looked over her shoulder, astounded at the light that now illuminated the area behind them. The male revue building was engulfed in flames, the glass of the windows crackling and popping as they shattered while orange and blue tongues licked their way towards the starlit sky.

Kendall gasped, covering her mouth with her hands. The speeding vehicle that had tried to run them over turned down an alleyway behind them and disappeared. Skye stopped the truck a safe distance away and turned to look back at the burning building as well. He was shocked. Dismayed. They could have been killed. First by the car determined to run them over, and then by the explosion.

"What's going on?" Kendall managed to find her voice enough to ask, although not really expecting an answer.

"I don't know. What did you do that someone is trying to kill you?"

"Me? I don't know. I've done nothing. I go nowhere, I don't know anyone. Why do you think it was me?" She was incredulous he asked such a thing.

"Because the car aimed for you specifically."

They both heard the sirens of the fire trucks coming to deal with the fire.

"My car is still there."

"We can't go back now. It's not secure. What if the person driving the other vehicle has a gun or something? Leave your car. It's probably not safe to retrieve at the moment. I don't think going to your house is, either."

"What? Why?"

"You have a license plate, right? A simple search on Google should be able to bring up your name and place of residence. If someone tried to kill you here, they might try so again at your house. It's not safe," he repeated, still looking behind to see if the car showed back up and they would have to begin the chase again.

"Then…maybe I should go to the police? What do I do?"

Skye was so glad she was not panicking. She spoke calmly, trying to analyze all the information on what was going on and, therefore, the best solution.

"I can take you to the police. Hell, I can drive you back to the fire trucks over there. I'm sure there are a couple of cops there, as well. They can send someone out to your house with you and make sure it's not dangerous. Maybe put a cop outside your house, just in case. However, I don't know what is going on, and you don't seem to either. So, how do we know whatever police you talk to is actually trustworthy? Or that they will even help when you don't even know why someone is after you? Fuck. This whole thing makes no sense." Skye ran a hand through his blond locks in frustration.

"Why would it matter? Listen. Thank you. You saved my life. You got me out of there before I was run over or blown up. Either way, I'm still alive as a result." She turned to look out the back window again. The flames were still burning hot, reaching towards the darkened sky.

It was moments like these she wished she could get the sage advice of her mom. Or just go over to her place and feel secure once again. Mothers always had a way of helping their children feel safe. At least, her mother did. Her mother was her best friend, her companion, her very reason for living. She was entirely lost without her.

"Do you have somewhere I can take you, other than your place? A trusted friend? A relative? Anyone?"

Kendall shook her head no; her lower lip started to quiver. Her whole life had revolved around her mother. As an only child, she had no siblings. Her father killed himself when she was only sixteen years old. For a long while, Kendall blamed herself for his suicide. She learned it was a natural response for children who were left behind to wonder what they might have done wrong or why they didn't see the symptoms of the intended to end their lives. It took a long while for her to accept her mother's explanation that it wasn't because of Kendall that her father ended his existence. More importantly, Kendall's mother loved her and would always be there for her. Never leave her. Right. Maybe the words should've been "leave her willingly". Her mother, Angela, fought with every breath she had to beat the cancer that ate her insides away. No matter what they did or how they tried, the vile curse of cancer still took her, leaving Kendall alone in a way she had never even dreamed possible.

Her mother was one of eight children, and all but one aunt survived. She was relatively close to her aunt; she certainly wouldn't go there to put her in danger just to feel safe. Besides, her aunt had a bad heart and a husband who wasn't faring well, either, with health issues of his own. Yes, she had cousins, but she was never very close to them. Her mother was the one who was the prominent one. She was a nurse who always cared for others, concerned for their well-being while Kendall remained the observer. Everyone loved her mother, while she mostly remained in the background, doing or fetching whatever her mother needed. Her cousins were married with families of their own and she was rarely invited to participate with their social gatherings, even before her mother passed away.

Now, it was even more of a strain, and instead of continuing her initial attempts to interact with her cousins more, too much time had passed to build up any kind of a stronger relationship with them. Even when she was invited to a special event, she was relegated to being with the older generation and remained silent and secluded and mostly alone even in the room full of people. It was an adjustment she had yet to reconcile with. She hated that when she gave any particular thought to her current circumstances, and especially when she thought of her mother, which was almost constantly, all she wanted to do was cry. She had never been so weak before she was alone. Ironic how her life changed within the beat of a heart.

She was suddenly drawn back to attention

when Skye reached around her to open the glove compartment and hand her a tissue from a small package he had in there. He must be used to dealing with emotional women to keep such an item in storage. He must also be used to them weeping as he didn't say anything about it while he offered her the small rectangle in order to wipe the pools from her eyes.

"Sorry. I don't mean to be such an emo, just still getting used to the loss."

"Did he pass away or did the bastard leave you?"

Kendall snorted softly at the statement and even quirked a slight smirk, putting the hand holding the tissue in her lap. "He was a she, and it was my mother. She'd been sick for a few years but the last few months were the worst for her. I've not quite gotten used to her being gone."

"I'm very sorry. Losing a mother has to be very hard, and when you are close as you seem to have been, it must be devastating."

"It truly is. She was my life. My world. I'm lost

without her. And because I spent so much time caring for her, I really don't have friends in times like this. I'm sure I'll be okay if you just take me back to my car. I don't mean to be a burden. You've been so very kind as it is."

"I really don't think it's wise for you to go home until tomorrow. In the daylight and with someone who can make sure everything is alright."

"Please. I'm sure it'll be fine. After all, the only way he or she would know where I lived would be if he followed me home, and I'll take all sorts of back roads to make sure I'm not being followed. I don't think he had enough time to get my license. He seemed too busy trying to run me down. Besides, I have a pet cat I should get home to."

Skye frowned, and she noticed when he did so, a couple of little lines over his forehead would appear. He simply nodded, but she could tell he was not at all happy about it. Turning the truck around, he headed back to the parking lot of the Cock-a-doodle. As he drove, he kept vigilance on the vehicles, just in case he spotted the one who chased them but a short while ago.

The fire engines were still hanging about, a few men in uniforms talking and making some notes. They had also been joined by a few police vehicles who were also talking to the firemen still gathered. She was surprised there were still so many around, even more surprised when she realized her car was no longer there. Skye realized it, too.

"Stay put. I'm going to talk to the cops and see where your car is."

Without waiting for an answer, he put the truck in park and hopped out of the cab while the engine was still running. The small group of men stopped talking and looked up at him as Skye approached. He was taller than most there, and shook hands with one of the firemen. Skye was fairly animated, talking with his hands and pointing here and there, and eventually gesturing to Kendall still sitting in the truck. She probably should get out, too, to see what was going on for herself, but the night's events drained her and she was perfectly content on letting Skye deal with it for her. She was also still a little tipsy from the second glass of wine she indulged in.

After a few more gestures and conversation, Skye shook the men's hands and returned to the cab, gracefully hopping in. *Must be those dancer moves that he does that so smoothly.*

Once he got back in and shut the door, he turned to face her. "They said that there were three cars in the lot and the police had them all towed. You won't be able to get your car out until tomorrow. I also told them what happened, and they want to talk to you. You can either come out with me and give them your statement and personal information now, or Officer Charles will come and get it from you. I wasn't sure what you felt up to. Then in a couple of days, once fire investigators do a bit more, well…investigating, they will want to talk to you further."

"I can go to them. Thank you." Kendall opened the door to slide out.

"I'll wait for you, then, and give you a ride."

"You don't have to do that. I appreciate all you've done for me, as it is. I wouldn't want to put you out further."

"You're putting me out if you don't let me make sure you're safe."

"How so?"

"Because I would be concerned the entire time that you got home safe and no one was there to harm you. I wouldn't get a moment's rest. I would be too agitated, and surely you wouldn't be as cruel as keeping me so worried about you when it could easily be avoided, now would you?"

Kendall had no good argument. She certainly didn't want to have him disquieted, especially about her, though why he would to begin with still astonished her.

Skye sensed her hesitation. "Go and talk to Officer Charles. I'll wait right here until you are finished and then we'll get you someplace secure for the night."

His tone brooked no nonsense, so she nodded and headed over to the group of men. She couldn't fathom why she felt like the lamb being led to the den of lions. Maybe because she wasn't used to men overall, or because they all watched her as if she were a virgin sacrifice, for some reason. She gave her head a quick shake to dispel such ridiculous thoughts. No wonder she became a writer; her imagination was all over the place.

Chapter Four

There were three policemen among the firemen in the semi-circle. She wasn't sure which one she was supposed to talk to, but as she got closer to the group, the middle male in the police uniform stepped towards her. She stopped directly in front of him, able now to see his name plate in the low light. Charles. He pulled out a notepad, but didn't open it yet.

"Ma'am. I'm Officer Charles. I would like to get your statement as to what occurred, as well as your information so we can contact you later. May I have your full name, please?"

"Sure. Kendall Roberts."

"Your address and phone?"

"123 Sycamore Lane. 555-9382"

"Can you tell me what happened?"

"I can try. Honestly, it happened so quickly, I'm still not sure about everything."

"Start from the beginning and take your time.

Try and remember as much detail as you can."

"Well, Skye…"

"Mr. Falcon?"

"Yes. Mr. Falcon walked me outside after the show. I thanked him for walking me out and said goodnight."

"Did you know Mr. Falcon before tonight?"

Kendall wasn't sure why that was important, but she respectfully answered anyway. "No. He is one of the dancers in the show. This is my first time having come here. He had pulled me up on stage for one of his numbers. I was reluctant to go, I might add. Then he asked if I would hang around after the show."

The entire time she was talking, the officer was making notes in his pad. He never looked up at her, just nodded for her to continue. "Go on."

"I wasn't going to wait around, but it was so crowded I decided to wait for the other guests to leave first. By the time they cleared the area, Skye—Mr. Falcon—was at my table and we started to talk. Anyways, once they started to shut the lights down, we stood to leave."

"You were going to leave together?"

"Goodness no. He was just escorting me outside. I said goodnight and proceeded to my car. Suddenly, I was face down on the cement, Mr. Falcon on top of me. A car had rushed towards me to hit me, I guess. I thought it was just a drunk driver or something. I really didn't have time to think about it. Skye—Mr. Falcon helped me to my feet, but then we realized the car was coming back at us again and we started to run away so as to not be killed by this vehicle. We managed to get into Mr. Falcon's truck and take off; the car followed us for a few minutes then vanished."

"Where were you when the car vanished?"

"In the cab of the truck."

Officer Charles rolled his eyes, then looked up from his notepad. "I meant what area?"

"Oh, sorry." She thought about it for a moment. "I am not entirely positive. It all happened so fast. I was sort of hanging on for dear life in the cab as Mr. Falcon sped away and I admit I was a bit in shock about everything. I think we may have lost the car about 90th and Central? Mr. Falcon might know better."

"I've already talked to Mr. Falcon and have his story."

"So you are trying to see if I can corroborate his version?"

"Something like that."

"Sorry, I really was plain scared and just too shocked this was happening to gather any useful information. Nothing like this has ever happened to me before. I mean, this is stuff you read in fiction novels and see on crime shows on television, not in real life."

"Sorry, ma'am, but this happens more often than you think."

"I'm stunned and amazed. I'm also sorry for you and your team that this is what you have to deal with more often than not."

"Did you see the car Mr. Falcon described?"

"Kind of. It was dark and speeding towards me, then chased after us. I didn't get a license plate or anything."

"Did you see a make, model or color of the car?"

"Not really well. It was a sports car, like a GTO or Mustang, but I'm not sure. Could've been a Corvette for all I know about makes and models. It was a dark color. Navy or black? The windows were tinted, that much I know 'cause I couldn't see the driver to know if I recognized them or not. I'm sorry. I'm not really much help at all. It just happened so fast and…" She paused a moment before repeating, "It just happened so fast."

"What about the explosion? Did you see anyone unusual before you went in or after you came out, before the car tried to run you over?"

"No, not really. But honestly, Officer, my mind was thousands of miles away. A parade could have walked in front of me, and I doubt I would have noticed."

"I'm sure we will have more questions, once the Fire Department finishes their investigation."

"Alright. I'm sorry I am not more help."

Officer Charles nodded noncommittally and turned his back on her as he continued to scribble down some notes, effectively dismissing her. She stood there a moment, unsure, but realized she had no choice but to return to Skye and the waiting Sierra.

When Skye realized she was finished talking to the police and headed back, he hopped out of the truck. He had opened the windows and turned the truck off while he waited for her to complete giving her statement. He went around to open the door and help her inside.

"Did you tell them everything?"

Kendall shrugged. "As much as I could. It all happened so quickly and it all feels so unreal. I keep waiting for Candid Camera to pop out and say I've been pranked."

"I wish it were something like that instead of someone trying to kill you for whatever reason unbeknownst to anyone but them. Are you sure you just didn't piss off an old boyfriend or something?"

"Positive. I've been pretty reclusive since my

mother passed, and prior to that I was extremely busy being her caretaker."

"We'll figure it out and keep you safe, as well."

"We? You don't have to do any of this. I mean, thank you for saving my life and all, but I don't want your life put at risk, either, just because you're trying to help me out of some sense of morality or something."

Skye leaned over her as she sat in the cab, a fierce look on his face. "Listen. I don't do anything I don't fucking want to do. This isn't some skewed sense of morality or anything else. I know I just met you, but I'm not going to just walk away and throw you to the wolves in the process. Whoever tried to run you over has also seen me and my truck. Probably got the license plate, too. I'm as much at risk now as you, and we'll have a better chance of getting through this together than apart."

Swallowing hard, Kendall nodded. "I'm sorry. I didn't mean it to sound so trivial. I sincerely do appreciate your assistance. I didn't even think about you being involved now. Goodness me, I'm so narrow minded and unobservant."

Skye pulled back, still holding open the door. "It's okay. I admit this has thrown me a bit, too. I can understand how confusing all this must be, as I feel the same way."

He stepped back and shut the passenger door before he walked around to the driver's side and climbed in. Once he was inside, he shut his door and started the truck.

"I think it's best if we stay together in one place tonight. Then tomorrow we can scope out your place and mine. However, until this is cleared up, I believe we should remain together just in case."

"Aren't we giving whoever is doing this easier access to get rid of us both at the same time if we stay together?"

"Probably. Or, we are making it harder if we are both paying attention and help each other out. If it is one guy, he can't strike us both at the same time."

"Ah. I hadn't thought of that. So if you are not

taking me to my place and we can't go to yours, where are you thinking? A hotel? What about my cat?"

"No. While you were talking to the cop, I called one of the other dancers. Raul said we could use his place. He is with some girl he met at the club so he won't be there tonight and before you freak out, there are three bedrooms in his place. Plus, he has a garage where I can hide the truck. Tomorrow, we will also worry about getting your car back. Surely your cat will be okay until tomorrow?"

"Yes. That is the nice thing about cats. They can be left alone for a day or so as long as they have food and water, and I made sure she had plenty of both before I left. I didn't want to be awakened early by a hungry fur-ball who had empty bowls as I figured I would be sleeping in." It was only at that moment that something dawned on her. "Oh, no. I dropped my phone and notepad when you pushed me down."

"Fuck. Since you are not carrying a purse, I

assume your license, credit cards and other personal shit were with the phone or notepad?"

"With the phone. The holder has a place for all that stuff."

"When we pick up your car tomorrow, we will file a police report about the missing phone. Was anything important in the notepad?"

"Not to anyone but me. I had my mother's card from her funeral and a couple of pictures of her, but mostly just notes on my next story. Nothing that can't be replaced, except the pictures."

"We will call the credit card companies to have them canceled when we get to Raul's."

"I don't have all the information."

"You won't need it. Give them your name and address and stuff, and they can find it."

Kendall remained quiet the rest of the drive. Her mind, however, was anything but inactive. It was going around and around in circles. Why would anyone want her dead? Did she see something she wasn't supposed to? Had she seen the person who blew up the club and not even realized it? It was the only thing that made any sense. They thought she saw something she shouldn't have and therefore she needed to die before she talked to anyone. She replayed the night's events since she left home to go to the club, but there was little to remember. Mostly, she was oblivious to almost everything, having the internal struggle of whether or not to go inside and thinking about how much she missed her mother. She hadn't paid attention to much of anything until the noise of the bridal party mixed with the cacophony of the birthday party drew her attention away from her own thoughts.

Did she see anything inside the club? Well, lots of screaming women and mostly naked men. Which, of course, was the whole point of her attending such an establishment. The only thing she thought unusual was the second glass of wine at her table when she returned from on stage.

"Did you order me another drink when you pulled me up on stage? Or is that like a policy, the girl that goes on stage gets a replacement drink?"

Skye cast his eyes over to her quickly then

returned them to the road, still checking the mirrors almost constantly to make sure they were not being followed. "No and no. Why?"

"When I got back from stage there was another glass of wine and my empty had been removed. I just figured you did it, or that it might be a way to thank the women who were brave or drunk enough to go on stage to have the men dance for them. I don't know. I though it strange, but then forgot about it until now."

"That is really odd. Unlike you, most women are thrilled or, as you say, drunk enough to be excited to be brought to the stage for a personal dance. The dances are their thank you for coming on stage." Skye frowned. None of the women would have bought her a drink, nor would any of the dancers. So where did the drink come from? "I'll talk to Monique tomorrow. I'll see if she knows who purchased it since she is the server who would have brought it. We will figure it out. I promise."

The whole night was bizarre as far as Skye was concerned. The only good thing coming out of it was he was getting to spend more time with Kendall. There was something about her, some sadness that haunted her eyes, an air of despair and uncertainty that drew him to her like a moth to a flame. Granted, she wasn't the most beautiful woman in the grand scheme of things, but outer beauty was not what interested him. He could have any supermodel he wanted, but it was the beauty of a heart and soul, of a gentleness, that caught his attention and captured his notice. To him, the fact she didn't really want to be at the club, that she tried to put distance between herself and the other vivaciously enthusiastic women who were definitely there to party and touch men they probably thought of as forbidden fruit or a last chance or once in a lifetime, was enticing. Maybe it was her wallflower approach to being there: sitting in the back and the lonely-yet-thoughtful way she watched the dancers, as if to memorize each fluid movement. At the time, he didn't understand why. He figured maybe she was a dancer and was looking to add new moves to her act, or a scout for some modeling or television agency scoping out some new talent. He never even dreamed of a writer. How sad she felt the need to explore men in a strip club instead of obtaining personal experience. But then, she was shy and reserved, something he instinctively discerned almost immediately.

She rebuffed him, in a kind way. Still it was a no to his subtle advances and he turned to leave with no way for him to find her again. At least until fate stepped in. Yes, he was totally a believer in fate. Cruel or kind, just or unjust, he believed in circumstances that led to his taking one path over the other and the resulting outcome. He wanted more time with her, a chance to get to know her better, and suddenly, fate stepped in, granting him his wish. He wasn't about to let her go as easily as she had dismissed him. Something told him this woman was who he needed to be with, for the moment at any rate. Tomorrow was always another day.

Chapter Five

Double checking the mirrors a few more times, he circled the block and pulled into a driveway. Hopping out, he headed to a keypad on the garage and punched in a few numbers he had written down, which he then stuck in his back jeans pocket. The garage door opened and Skye hurried back to the truck, pulling in and turning off the engine before he closed the garage doors.

"The door connecting the garage to the house should be open. Go on in. I want to keep an eye out here for a couple more minutes. Make sure we weren't followed. Though with all the twists and turns I did, I would be surprised if someone managed without setting off my Spidey senses."

Kendall slipped out of the passenger side of the truck and went into the house. "Should I turn lights on or stay in the dark until you have assessed the threat level?"

"Turn them on. That might bring out a threat if

I didn't see it already. Better to be safe than sorry."

Kendall followed his instructions and flipped on a couple of the lights. She found herself in a small foyer that led into a utility room complete with a washer and dryer. That room opened into the kitchen where she searched for even more lights. One room led into another and she kept turning on lights until the entire lower floor was illuminated.

Only then did she return to the kitchen and wait for Skye. This whole thing was unbelievable, and she kept waiting for the hidden cameras to show up. Why would anyone want her dead? It just didn't make sense. Now she was in someone else's home, hiding. And with a drop-dead gorgeous male as well. She was sure he wanted to be anywhere else other than here, with his life on the line.

Skye shut the door to the garage behind him as he came in. "I didn't see anyone else. I think we are safe, but we should shut all the drapes and curtains." He had already moved to the kitchen window, closing the rose-and-lace decorated curtains. "I'm going to have to tease the hell out of

Raul for the frilly decorating he's got going on around here."

Skye turned around, taking a good look at Kendall. She looked harried, and he knew all of this must be hard on her. He pulled open the fridge. "How about a beer? Or, I could see if he has something stronger around here if you want? I know I sure could use a drink after all of this."

"A beer would be good. Or something stronger. Doesn't matter."

"A beer to start and I'll look around to see if there is anything stronger. I think we can both use something stiffer than a water-downed beer." Skye looked at the label, giving it a distasteful glare. "Never even heard of this brand before. With the money we make at the club, he could at least drink something respectable."

"The beer is fine. My stomach is a bit upset, anyways. My head is still swimming, as well. There is just so much going on, so much I don't understand."

"I know. It can't be easy. None of this can.

Listen, why don't you sit and write down whatever you remember or people who you could consider as enemies. This way, you will have a head start when the police are ready to talk to you with more questions. In the meantime, I am going to check out the rest of the house. Make yourself at home." Skye headed out and up the stairs to the second floor bedrooms. It was his loud whoop, which caused Kendall to literally fall off the stool she was sitting on and run up the stairs in a panic.

Skye was standing in the doorway of the room at the end of the hall. All the other doors were opened, but Kendall paid little attention to them. He must have heard her approach, because he turned around laughing. "You have got to see his bedroom. Oh my fucking god. I am so taking pictures. Where is my phone? No one is ever going to believe me without photographic evidence."

Kendall peered into the room. Skye was right. It was astonishing, like something out of a bachelor pad from the Eighties. The room was decorated in a tiger print, with a mirror above the bed. There were dark drapes on the window and… Kendall had to look twice. Naked wallpaper on the walls? Of the Kama Sutra? Kendall put her hand to her mouth in astonishment while Skye remained in the hallway bowed over with laughter. Finally, calming down enough, he went back inside to snap a couple of photos. "No one is going to believe this."

"I admit it is pretty funny. I'm not sleeping in here. Just saying."

Putting his camera phone away, Skye nodded. "I'm not either, but I found two other bedrooms down this hallway and both are decent enough. Take whichever one you want and I'll take the other. I'm going to go lock up a few things downstairs. Make sure all the windows and doors are locked. You going to be okay by yourself?"

"I've been by myself for quite a while. I'm sure I'll manage." Kendall headed down the hall looking into the various rooms, now that she wasn't running to Skye in a panic.

The first room from the master bedroom was decorated more simply but with dark, rich, walnut colors. She then moved to the next open door and saw it was a bathroom. *Good to know,* she thought. Continuing further down, the next room was a storage room of some sort. The final room, and the one closest to the stairs, was decorated in a pale blue with oak furniture. It was light and airy and suited her needs. She still felt strange being in another's home, but dire circumstances required doing things one normally wouldn't do.

Entering the room, Kendall moved to the window and peered out.

"Get away from the window, Kendall. Nothing is secure at the moment and we don't need to take unnecessary risks."

Kendall pulled the curtains closed before she moved away from the window as Skye had instructed her while he leaned against the doorjamb, his arms folded over his barrel chest.

"This room suits you. A good choice. Do you need anything? I think you should get some sleep. We still have to deal with your car and everything tomorrow and it's already been a hectic night."

"Where will you be?"

"Not in the sex room, that's for sure. Actually, I decided I'm going to sleep on the couch downstairs. Make sure nothing else happens, and it's a better vantage point than up here. Unless, of course, you would like me to stay with you?" Skye gave her an appreciative appraisal. Despite the risk, he would love to take her in his arms and spend the night making her scream or moan in unadulterated pleasure.

Kendall felt almost naked under his scrutinizing gaze. There was a moment, brief though it was, she almost caved into the lasciviousness of her own burning desire. However, she realized he wouldn't be interested in anything other than a quick, impersonal lay and she didn't want to be another notch on his bedpost. "I'll be fine alone. The couch? Surely you need as much rest as I do. After all, you did all that dancing tonight, amongst everything else."

Skye gave her a smirk. "I'm used to little sleep. There are towels in the closet by the bathroom. I'm sure there is a shirt or something in one of the drawers you can borrow to sleep in. Call me if you need anything else, otherwise I'll see you in the morning." Skye backed out of the room, shutting the door on her. She didn't even get a chance to say goodnight.

He headed down the stairs, turning out all the lights as he went. He couldn't help but think of the woman upstairs. He was impressed by her. Through everything, she didn't whine or complain. She was level headed. When given the chance, she turned him down. Him! He couldn't ever remember a time when a woman said no to being with him, even if it was just for a drink or more conversation.

Ironic how fate intervened. Positive he would never see her again as she headed to her car in the club's lot, he was thrown in her path in order to protect her. And now, they were going to rest under the same roof, even if not the same bed. It would give him time to get to know her better, even though he didn't understand the deep desire and need to do so. She was just a woman. Why did it matter if he got to know her or not? Was it because she intrigued him so? Because she didn't just fall at his feet? Because she came to the club for something other than a cheap thrill? Maybe it was her sadness that draped across her shoulders that captured his imagination. Maybe it was her moral integrity. Whatever it was, it was something he hadn't felt in years, if ever.

Getting settled, he laid on the couch, listening to her upstairs. He heard her go into the bathroom, heard the water in the shower, heard the door of the bedroom close and then nothing more. The house was quiet outside of the ticking of the grandfather clock in the living room. He should be exhausted. Asleep. Yet, he was wide awake just thinking about the woman who was sleeping above his head. Yeah, this was going to be a really long night.

Chapter Six

Kendall awoke in the strange bedroom, and it took her a few minutes to recall where she was and why she was there. The smell of coffee and bacon wafted up to her. She stretched and looked at the digital clock by the bedside. 10:31. She couldn't remember the last time she slept that late. Sure, she went to bed late. It was after 2 a.m. before she settled down enough to get any sleep.

Getting out of bed and dressed, she headed down to the kitchen where the delicious smells were emanating from. She stopped dead in her tracks, watching Skye shirtless, cooking eggs and bacon on the stove. The muscles in his back bunched and released as he moved fluidly about the kitchen, unaware she was watching. She wondered what those muscles would feel like under her fingertips or what he would feel like under her. She gave herself a mental shake and entered the room, wishing him a good morning.

"Good morning, beautiful. Coffee is ready over there, and breakfast will be ready in a few minutes. I hope scrambled eggs are okay."

"Coffee is perfect and so are scrambled eggs. Thank you." She ignored the beautiful remark. He was just being nice and she didn't need an argument this early in the day. Pouring herself a cup of joe, she sat on the stool. "Did you sleep okay?"

Skye nodded while he added eggs and bacon to a plate, placed it in front of her, then turned to prepare another for himself. In truth, he barely slept at all. Dozed mostly, listening to the odd noises and making sure none were threatening. Trying desperately to not think of the woman upstairs and having to shift himself in order to feel a bit more comfortable when he did think of her. "You?"

"I had a bit of trouble falling asleep, new place and all. But once I did, I slept really good."

"I'm glad."

When the sound of keys jingled in the door, Skye pulled her off the stool and shoved her behind him, grabbing the chopping knife in his hand defensively.

A man Kendall recognized from the previous evening came in, but stopped with his arms raised when he noticed Skye holding a knife. "Whoa, dude. This is how you greet someone who let you stay here?"

Skye relaxed, putting the knife back down. "Sorry, man. It's been a crazy night."

Raul came the rest of the way in, shutting the door behind him. He gave a look to Kendall, his dark brown eyes giving her an appraising look. He was tall, albeit shorter than Skye. He was also loaded with muscles, but a six pack and not an eight. He was a bit leaner than Skye, but he was also good looking. Just not that clean, business look Skye pulled off, but rather a more rugged, Mexican cowboy. He held his hand out to her. When she gave him her hand, he bowed over it and kissed her knuckles.

"I hope you found my abode enjoyable." The way he said "enjoyable" made her feel dirty. Suddenly, she wanted another shower. A dozen, even. She tried to overlook the feeling and convince herself it was just the culmination of everything that happened in the last twelve hours or so.

"I found it restful. Thank you for allowing us to use it."

Skye stepped up to him, handing him a cup of coffee. "We need to talk. Privately. Kendall, finish your breakfast. I'll be right back."

Turning back to her food, Kendall let the two men head into the living room to discuss their business, which she was positive included her. She was unsure how much Skye told him last night when he requested the use of Raul's place.

Skye followed Raul into the other room. "Thanks again for letting us crash here."

"I'm still not understanding why, dude. You have a really nice place of your own. She that clingy you didn't want her to know where you lived after you screwed her? That's why you go to their place, dude. Fuck 'em and leave 'em."

"It's not like that, you ass. We couldn't go to her place or mine because it wasn't safe. Man, some major shit went down last night. The club burned down, someone tried to run her over, someone chased us in their car. It was freaky crazy."

Raul drew his eyes together in angst. "What the fuck you mean the club burned down? What the fuck is going on, dude?"

Skye shrugged. "It's what I'm saying. Last night was a major cluster fuck and I've got no fucking clue what's going on. There was a bomb or something. I was walking Kendall out of the joint when I saw this car veer towards her at top speed. It was aiming right for her. Stupid ass. I figured it was a drunk who just didn't see her or something. Then, it headed back, and aimed for her again, only this time I was with her.

We got into my truck and took off. It followed us for a bit. Then this huge boom went off and shook my truck. Looking in the mirror, I could see something burning back in the direction of the club. It was pretty awesome, in a way. Flames were like ten feet high.

When we felt sure the car was no longer

following us, I headed back to the club. The fire department was there. The cops towed her car from the lot to give the trucks more room to maneuver. I figured whoever was after her got her address from either her wallet or her license and assumed they would get my address from my plate, having followed it for a bit. I just couldn't take the chance and didn't want to go to a hotel."

"Makes sense. Glad I could help in offering you the place. Shit, that does sound messed up, though." Raul rubbed his chin in thought. "So, was she at least a good lay to make all this worth it?"

Skye snarled. "The woman was attacked and the club burned, so we are now out of a job and you are worried about if I fucked her last night?"

Raul smiled. "Yes, 'cause if she was, I might want to take a try at her myself."

Skye moved lightning fast, grabbing Raul by the collar and pushing him up against a wall. "Don't even think it, dude. She's a nice lady with a ton of shit on her plate and she doesn't need an insensitive asshole to fuck her and kick her to the curb. She's not going to be another conquest for you. You hear me?"

Raul raised his hands defensively. "Yeah, man. Yeah. I get it. Hands off, she's yours. Damn, she must be rocking. Ain't seen you this worked up about a woman in like fucking ever."

Skye pushed him back, then let him go, running a hand through his blond locks. "Yeah. Surprises me, too, but she's nice and she doesn't deserve to be treated like crap."

"Got it, man. Hands off."

Skye wished keeping his hands off would be all it would take, but he doubted if Kendall would have him, either. There was still the slight thought she wasn't into men at all, that maybe she batted for the other team. It truly was the only thing that made any credible sense to him.

"Come on. Breakfast is getting cold. Thanks again for letting us use your crib."

"No problem."

The two men walked back into the kitchen. Skye fixed another plate for Raul, then sat to eat his own breakfast, which he had plated just as Raul had come back home. The three ate in silence for a few minutes, the men shoveling their food in while Kendall had finished hers and was sipping her coffee watching them.

Chapter Seven

Finishing up their breakfast, Kendall cleaned up while the men continued to talk. When she completed washing everything and putting it in the drying rack, she brought her coffee over to where the two men were sitting as they made various phone calls. As she approached, they each completed their phone calls, hanging up.

"I just got off the phone with Michael. Of course, the police and fire department had talked to him about his property, but he didn't know there were witnesses, more or less. As in Kendall and me. He said he was contacting the other dancers today and after he talks to the insurance company, he'll schedule a meeting to discuss what's going to happen. He's supposed to meet the fire chief in a couple of hours to go over the damage."

Raul sat back, stretching his legs out and crossing them at the ankle. "Fine and dandy for folks like you, Skye, who don't have to worry about having only one source of income. What the fuck are the rest of us supposed to do?"

"I guess that info will come at the staff meeting he'll schedule at a later time."

Kendall wondered what else Skye did for finances after Raul's comment.

"I have a mortgage to pay, and alimony and child support. I need the money."

"Get off my back, dude. I didn't set the place on fire. In case this might have escaped your notice, Kendall and I were almost killed. Which, I might remind you, is why we stayed here at your place." Skye stood, turning to Kendall. "Are you about ready to go? We have a dozen things to do today, starting with getting your car back."

"Yes. Of course." Kendall picked up her coffee cup, putting it into the sink and turned to Raul. "Thank you for letting us stay here last night. I am very appreciative. Pleasure meeting you."

Skye headed through the kitchen to the entrance of the garage and opened the door for her. Once she was in and buckled up, he walked around the front and climbed in the driver's seat. Raul had followed them and pushed a button on the wall to open the door. Only then did Skye start up his truck and back out. Kendall waved to Raul; he nodded and pushed the button again to shut the door, blocking himself from their view. She was glad they were leaving. Raul seemed nice enough; yet something about the way he looked at her like she was prey, or the intonations of his voice, set the hairs on the nape of her neck to prickling with concern.

"I thought we would stop at the fire department first. I need to talk to them about a few things. Then we can see about getting your car from the impound lot. After which, I'll follow you home and make sure everything is kosher. We should also check in with the police, too."

"I think I'll be okay once I get my car."

"No way, chick-a-dee. The guy who tried to run you down definitely had the opportunity to get your license plate and possibly your phone, driver's license and lord knows what else. Which is why we also need to make a stop at the station."

"I really don't want to take up your day like this. I'm sure you have many other things to do than follow me around all day."

Skye threw her a glance before his eyes returned to the road. "Even if I did, which I don't, but even if I did, it wouldn't matter. You're my priority now."

"Why? I mean. Well, yeah, why?"

Skye smirked. "You just are. So forget about it and accept it. First stop, the station." *I'm not letting you get away,* he thought silently. *I'm a lot of things, but my momma didn't raise me to be a fool, and I would be the biggest fool around if I let you walk out of my life, even if I don't fully understand this need I have for you to be in it.*

Kendall gave him a perplexed look. She had always cared for others, especially her mom. No one had cared for her since she was a child, and the fact he wanted to make sure she was okay when he didn't even know her, flabbergasted her in a multitude of ways.

Minutes later, Skye pulled around the back of the Moraine Valley Fire House and parked. The town of Moraine Valley was a fairly small one. The population only 5,000. As a result, there was only one police station, one hospital and one fire station.

"You parked in the employee lot. Should I wait?"

"I am aware. No. Don't wait in the car. Come on in and meet the guys."

"Meet the guys? You know them here?"

"Yeah. I do some part-time work for them. I'm a POC firefighter."

"POC? What is that?"

"It means paid on call. We used to be volunteers, but they were losing a lot of men who figured volunteering was not as important as a paid job, so they either became employees full time or quit. This was a way to get men to still volunteer but make it worth their time. It also enabled the POC to keep other jobs as well. We can do anything as long as it is not illegal, like selling drugs or being part of the mob or something."

"Is that what Raul meant about you having another source of income?"

"Yeah. Come on." Skye hopped out of the cab of the truck and ran to open her side of the door. She didn't need to know about his wealthy inheritance. He didn't want to be liked for his money, so he never shared that information with anyone. Assisting her out of the cab, he led her to the back door and opened it for her. It took a moment for her eyes to adjust. By the time they did, Skye had her by the elbow and was gently leading her down a hall to some offices. They passed some of the firemen along the way, and Skye said hello to all of them by name but didn't stop until he reached an office with the words Fire Investigator: Barney Osnike inscribed on the doorplate.

Skye knocked. A deep voice told them to enter, and Skye opened the door, holding it for Kendall. They entered the office, where an older man sat behind a large Formica desk. He was mostly bald with a bit of short, grey hair around the base of his head. He also had a thick, grey mustache and a bit of a beer belly, but by no means was he fat.

Skye moved in front of Kendall as he reached forward with his hand extended. Barney stood, taking Skye's hand and shaking it. Barney looked questioningly at Kendall. Turning to her, Skye introduced them.

"Barney? This is Ms. Kendall Roberts. Kendall, this is our fire investigator, Barney. Ms. Roberts was witness to the club burning down last night."

Kendall shook Barney's hand, then they all sat down. Barney steepled his hands. "I suppose you are here for prelim info."

"Yeah. Ms. Roberts and I were almost killed last night, so you could say I have a vested interest in this investigation."

Barney nodded, then turned to his computer, punching up a few different screens before he found the one he was looking for. Skye moved around to hover behind him to see the screen better.

"As you can see from these pictures taken at the scene, the fire started in the storage room. From the radius pattern, it appears to have spread outward from the initial blast."

"Michael can check this, but I'm pretty sure there was a delivery last night. I remember he was complaining the truck was late, and then when the show started he was complaining again. You might want to check with him, though, just to be sure."

"He is on my list for interviews later today. I left a message for him to get back to me just a few minutes ago."

"Did you find a cause at the point of origin?"

"There were some remains of a timer and some chemical residue. They have been sent to the state lab for testing. As usual, it's going to take 48 hours or more if they are busy. You know how our little town is low priority, unless they are bored or Bill gets on their asses."

Bill was Bill Hopkins, the town's mayor and a very boisterously influential male. He had the ear of the governor, mostly because he was the governor's brother-in-law and they got together weekly at the governor's mother's home for Sunday dinner. So one didn't want to piss off Bill without possibly getting the short side of the proverbial governor stick rammed up any unmentionable locations. It certainly was not a good thing to be on the receiving end of. Period.

"Thanks, Barney. Keep me up-to-date when you hear back from the state?"

"Sure. I will." Barney stood to see the two of them out.

Skye looked at his phone, punched a couple of the buttons, then put it in his back pocket again. Just as they were headed out the door of the station, the alarms went off and all the men came running from various doors to head towards the trucks. Skye pulled Kendall back and out of the way, then ran behind a couple of them.

He stopped with Kendall right behind him as the address of the fire they were being sent on came through the radio. 123 Sycamore Lane. Skye turned to Kendall when he heard her gasp. Quickly, he moved to her side. "You okay?"

"That's my house." Kendall managed to get out, totally stunned.

"Fuck." Skye called out, "Barney, I'm going to meet you there. Taking my own truck and bringing the owner of the house."

"I have a cat inside. They have to save her. Please."

"Barney, be advised one cat inside the home."

"Affirmative."

Chapter Eight

The GMC Sierra followed the fire trucks, as long as they didn't go through any red lights. When they did, Skye would catch up to them as best he could once he got the green go-ahead. They arrived at her small bungalow not too long after the firefighters, who were still unloading their equipment.

Kendall hopped out as soon as he stopped the truck and ran towards the front door. Skye quickly followed her and pulled her back. "They know to look for your cat."

"I'm worried they won't find her. She gets scared easily and will hide under a piece of furniture or in my closet."

"You can't go in there, but…let me put on some equipment and I will go in looking for her specifically. Would you stay here if I do that?"

Kendall nodded, her eyes pleading for him to help, even if she couldn't vocalize it.

"Stay out of the way." Without another word, he dashed over to his truck and started to pull out a fire suit from the back. Quickly slipping it on, he grabbed a helmet and spoke to the fire chief as he dashed into the house. He didn't even know the cat's name or color or anything, but he had to find it. For her. The cat couldn't be that dumb it would stay in a closet or something just to burn to death, could it? He never had a cat. A dog once, but even that was years ago.

He checked the rooms, especially the closets, and sure enough, the third one he looked into there were a pair of eyes looking at him. Skye reached out and grabbed the little fur ball, scooping it into his arms. As he turned about to head out of the room, he heard the creaking sound of the floor wanting to give away from the heat and intensity of the fire. He didn't waste time. As he ran out, through the microphone in his helmet, he warned the other fire fighters in the house while he jumped over a hole which suddenly appeared before him. He never let the cat go, who clung to him with her claws. She seemed to know he was trying to help save her life and therefore didn't try to run away.

Skye made it outside just as portion of the house collapsed in upon itself. He turned around stunned at the damage the house was taking. It was burning way too hot. From what he could see inside while he was in there for that brief time, it indicated to him it was not a natural fire, but one set using accelerants. As to what kind would be up to Barney and the team of forensics at the state labs. However, Skye was pretty sure the same thing that had been used on the fire at the club was used at Kendall's home and therefore most likely set by the same person. Skye was not one for coincidence and this was too much of a similarity even for him.

Kendall was by his side almost instantaneously once he was clear of the burning abode.

"Tinkerbell! Oh my god, you're safe. Thank you. Thank you so much for finding her and getting her out." Kendall hugged the feline close to her after taking her from Skye's arms. Kendall was almost in tears with relief.

Skye removed his personal protection equipment and returned it to its storage location. By the time he finished, Officer Charles approached him. Kendall stayed out of the way of those who were working so diligently in trying to salvage anything they could, or at least prevent it from spreading to the other houses in the neighborhood.

With Tinkerbell safe in her arms, everything else could be replaced, except for her mother's things. She knew they were just things, but it was hard to say goodbye to the only tangible items she had from her mother. Again, that loneliness of her mother being gone hit her hard. She wept softly in Tinkerbell's fur, a combination of relief and loss.

Skye and the police liaison for the fire department shook hands.

"Hey, Brett. What do you think of this?"

"I don't think it's an unrelated happenstance. Barney is going to get some samples when it's safe and a full investigation is going to be underway, but

I have a feeling the lab is only going to tell us what you and I already suspect. This was set by the same perp who torched the Cock-a-doodle last night. It is rare, though, to see an arsonist move from fires to attempted murder."

"I was thinking the same thing. The only thing I can assume is Kendall saw him and he figures he needs to silence her before she remembers."

"She didn't seem to remember much, overall. I assume she was just a bit drunk from being at the show."

Skye rubbed his chin in thought, sending a glance over to Kendall cuddling her cat.

"Maybe, but she seemed a bit off when I met her after the show. We talked about it a bit, and she says after she returned from the stage there was a full glass of wine at her table. Understand, she was sitting in the back by herself. Monique would not have technically serviced it. Usually they would have to go to the bar themselves to get their drinks, unless they were on the main floor."

"Have you talked to Monique about this?"

"Not yet. We were going to get her car from the impound lot, then head over to see Monique and Michael. I wanted to talk to both of them about the delivery truck and her second drink. Unless she is a true lightweight, I can't imagine two glasses of wine making her reflexes so off. I may be jumping the gun here, but I really think she was given a spiked drink. Something that affected her motor coordination as well as her memory. It would make sense if the perp slipped her a Mickey in order to get her to forget whatever it is she saw that would condemn him."

"Makes a hell of a lot of sense to me." Brett scribbled down a few things in his notepad. "Where are you two staying?"

"Well considering she just lost her home, I was going to see if she wished to stay at my pad for a few days."

"We should probably check it out as well, since the perp got your truck plates and maybe more during your chase last night."

"Man, I would really appreciate that. Once I

can get her inside, I can set the house alarm and know she is safe from this lunatic."

"I'll contact Chavez and have him bring the bomb sniffing dogs just to be sure. I'm not sure what to expect from this guy, but I'm not about to take any chances. This is getting serious like a heart attack. I don't want this perp to have any more opportunities than possible."

"We were planning on getting her car out of impound. Should we do so or wait?"

"If I were you? I'd wait. The car is safe there. He can't track it if it ain't moving. And if he has had access to it, better it be at the impound lot than at your house. I'll also put in a request to have an officer stationed outside, just to be safe."

"Unmarked. If the perp sees the squad, he might figure he is in the right place or something. I don't want any unnecessary chances to be taken, if possible."

"I'll talk to the captain, but that is up to him." Brett Charles turned back to the burning building. "Seems as if it is almost out. Not much more you or her can do today. Can't get in until it's been cleared by the investigators, and that is going to take at least 24 hours. Let me call a car to see you home." He nodded to Kendall, still holding Tinkerbell tightly, and headed to his car to call dispatch.

Chapter Nine

Kendall and Skye leaned against his truck as they waited for Chavez and his team to clear Skye's home. Skye had given them his keys so they could let themselves in while he made a quick stop at the local store for Kendall to get whatever items she was going to need, especially for Tinkerbell. She hadn't wanted to wait in the truck, but she stood by the window so Tinkerbell wouldn't feel like she was abandoned.

They had barely spoken since she climbed into the cab and he asked her if she wished to stay with him until things got sorted out. Skye added the police thought it would be safer than if she were to stay alone in a hotel, and since she already told him last night that she didn't have any friends she could turn to, it made sense for Kendall stay with him. She agreed, albeit somewhat reluctantly.

Skye glanced at Kendall as she held Tinkerbell as if she were a lifeline. Although, Skye couldn't really blame Kendall. She had been through so much as it was, with the attempted hit and run, her car being impounded, and her house burning with everything in it except her pet. Skye was well aware she was still mourning the loss of her mother on a very deep, emotional level. She was probably still in shock about the entirety of the situation, which was why she was quiet. He was willing to give her some time to adjust.

Now, standing outside as they waited for Chavez to give them the all clear sign, Skye spoke softly, though he didn't look at her as a way of still giving her some semblance of privacy. "I'm sorry all this is happening to you. I'll do what I can to help keep you safe. I know this is a lot to take in. I understand you are still dealing with the loss of all your stuff from your house, but we got the most important thing, Tinkerbell, out safely. Surely, it's something you can be thankful for?"

Kendall nodded. She was trying to deal with all of it. He was being more than kind, but there was no way he could understand her emotional state. It was all she could do to hold it together. They may have been just material items to most people, but to her, they were the only legacy she had left. The only tie to her mother, and even her father, that remained after their deaths, and she was left alone. Now, it was all gone. Every shred of her past, of her life, had disappeared in burning flames. The arsonist took more from her than he could've imagined. The proverbial rug had been pulled out from under her and she felt even more alone than ever before, despite how impossible it was to even contemplate.

She hadn't been ready to let those materialistic things, which belonged to her mother, go just yet. They were the tangible ties of all that remained of a time Kendall felt loved, protected and safe. Kendall missed the security her mother brought; she was her best friend, the shoulder she could cry on, the person she could talk to about anything. All of it was gone, and a huge, empty blackhole remained, sucking whatever emotions and sanity Kendall had left.

It was akin to losing her mother all over again

and she still had not regrouped from that. She wanted to move past those last few weeks of her mom in the hospital undergoing surgeries, biopsies and treatments. How much weight she had lost in the process. How she dreaded seeing the doctors come in at the end with nothing but bad news about her mother's declining health and the progression of the cancer spreading from her breast, to her lungs, to her colon and finally her bladder. There was nothing left of her mother at that point, certainly no quality of life.

Despite all the fighting her mother did, she was up against a powerful force and on the losing side. Her mother tried desperately to hang on, but Kendall knew it was time to tell her to go find her peace in death. As hard as it was to make that decision and tell her mother it was okay to leave her mortal skin behind for a better place, Kendall regretted it each and every moment of every day.

She wanted to be selfish and hold onto her mother just a little longer. She wanted to tell her mom not to go and leave her with no one in this world who cared or even noticed she was alive, but she didn't. Without quality of life, she knew her mother would not want to live, and Kendall wouldn't be able to blame her. She did the sensible thing, the unselfish thing. All she had left were the things her mother used, wore and collected. Now, even they were gone. Kendall didn't know how to deal with such an overwhelming loss. To others they may have been materialistic items, but to her, they were all the connective ties she had left in this world.

Skye reached out to her to pull her in a hug and offer his comfort. Kendall pulled back immediately. Holding in her tears was no longer a viable option as they streamed down her cheeks.

"Don't. You have no idea, none. To you it was stuff. To you it was just banausic possessions, which can be replaced with insurance and whatever, but it was more than that to me. Don't get me wrong. I am very grateful for you getting Tinkerbell out. If I had lost her, too, I don't know what I might have done."

Skye felt the rebuff and, normally, something like that would turn him off and he would head as quickly as possible in the other direction. Not with Kendall. What was it about her that enticed him so? That made him want to hold her close and protect her from the big, bad, nasty world? He didn't need her, or any woman for that matter. Too untrustworthy. Too emotional. Basket cases, that's what they were. Unpredictable and not respectful to any who might actually give a damn. *Bitter much?* he silently asked himself.

Yet, Kendall made him feel differently and he wasn't sure why. Hell, he didn't even really know her, but there was that sense of helplessness mixed with strength that clearly caught his attention. He wanted to know everything about her. He wished to find out if she was as pure and kindhearted as she appeared, or as shy. She had such an inner strength about her that it still astounded him. Her rebuke only made her more interesting to him.

"If you want to talk, I'm a really good listener."

"Thanks. You have done so much already. I am

very grateful." Kendall quickly wiped her cheeks and looked up as Chavez approached the two of them.

"It's all clear, Mr. Falcon. You can go in now. An unmarked car will be parked outside and we will also have a roaming marked vehicle swing by often to parlay any suspicion from the unmarked one."

"Thank you. I appreciate knowing we are in such secure hands."

Chavez left the two of them. Skye got the bags of items recently purchased as Kendall retrieved Tinkerbell from the cab. The small calico appeared to be calmer once she was in Kendall's arms. The whole ordeal was traumatic for a person, but for an animal ever more so.

Skye led Kendall into the house and shut the door behind them, then led her to her room. Setting the bags on the bed, Skye backed up. "Why don't you rest and get settled a bit, then I will show you around the house if you want. It's been a very eventful day, and I am sure the two of you need time to adjust. If you need anything, just holler. I only ask one thing of you. Don't go into the basement for any reason. It's really a mess down there and I would hate to have you hurt. It's the door by the kitchen at the base of the stairs."

"Sure. That won't be a problem. Thanks again." Kendall followed him back to the door and stopped him with her free hand since Tinkerbell occupied her other arm. "I know I have not really said anything, and what I have, doesn't seem adequate enough, but I am eternally grateful for you saving not only my life, but also Tinkerbell's." She leaned in and gave him a quick hug before stepping back.

"Glad to be of assistance." He gave her a smile that made her heart skip a beat before he shut the door, affording her some privacy to get settled in the guest room.

Chapter Ten

Skye headed downstairs, pulling out his phone. The first call he made was to Michael Walso, the owner of Cock-a-doodle Male Revue.

"Michael here."

"Hi, Mike. It's Skye."

"Yeah? What do you need?"

"Listen, man. Sorry about the club burning."

"Yeah. Me, too. Fucking sucks pig's balls. Is that what you are calling about? Work?"

"No. Actually, I was wondering if you had a chance to talk to either the fire chief or Barney, the investigator."

"Not yet. I have an appointment to see a Mr. Osnike, from the fire department, later today."

"That's Barney the investigator. He will probably bring along Officer Charles, since they are working together on this."

"I hope they sign my papers for the insurance company. I want to get the claims made as soon as possible so I can either tear down and rebuild or refurbish. I am unsure how much damage there is or what the insurance will cover. I just hope they don't think I am the one who started it. Then I will never get paid."

"I told them about the problems you had with the delivery truck yesterday. They are probably going to question you on that, as well."

"Shitass paperwork burned up with the place. I'll have to call the delivery companies to have them forward the documentation."

"Actually, that's why I was calling. I was hoping you could tell me a bit more about what happened with the delivery."

"Why?"

"Let's just say, I am doing a bit of my own investigation."

Stillness on the line, then a huff of breath. "Fine. Cecil was supposed to be there at four to unload. I waited around for hours. I called the office and all they kept saying was he should be there. Then at about six when I was blowing my top, their office said he was having truck problems and would be there as soon as possible. The truck showed up at 10:30, when the show was about to begin. And it wasn't Cecil. It was some dude I didn't know. I let him in the storage room to unload, and then had to deal with an issue out on the floor. One of the bridesmaids kept trying to go backstage to see the guys fully naked. Bitch. Anyways, he was gone by the time I came back to find him. I hadn't even signed the paperwork or checked the stock of what he delivered before he was gone. The chief last night told me they suspected it was started in the storage room. Makes me think the asswad brought it in with the rest of the gear. What he has against my place, I sure as hell don't know."

"Me, either, Mike. But thanks for the info. I appreciate it."

"Yeah. No problem. Anything else?"

"No. I'll talk to you later. See what the insurance has to say and then let me and the guys know what you are going to do. I know with Raul and some of the others, this is their only source of income."

"Yeah. I know. It stinks of skunk piss all the way around. I'll let you guys know what is going on when I get things nailed down."

"Great. Thanks." Skye disconnected the call and tapped his phone against his leg. So not only was the truck late, it wasn't even the normal delivery guy. Skye glanced up at the wall clock. It was 4:52 p.m. Making the decision, he dialed the phone.

"Hello?"

"Monique?"

"Yeah?"

"Hey, Moan. It's Skye."

"Finally calling for that date?"

Monique has been after him, since he got hired a few months back, to be her boyfriend. Sometimes she was a bit too aggressive for his taste. And way too scrawny. Like a walking twig, as far as he was concerned. He wouldn't doubt it if someone told him she was anorexic. At times, Skye even found her attentions a bit too amorous. He liked self-assured women, what guy didn't? But wanting to get into his pants on day one was a bit much, making him feel like a piece of meat. Another reason why he liked Kendall. She looked at him, not as a dancer, or a stripper, or even as a male, but as a person. Someone who had concerns, feelings, and more to offer than just a good lay. Actually, Kendall hasn't even indicated she wanted sex with him and that was something new and different. It intrigued him further.

"No, Moan. Not calling about a date. Calling to ask you a couple of questions, if you don't mind."

"Not at all, sexy. Ask away."

"Do you remember the woman that sat in the back of the club last night?"

"Oh. Isn't that awful, about the club, I mean. I can't believe it burned down. Think Michael did it for the insurance?"

"No. I don't. A lot of guys, including you, are now out of work. Michael isn't like that, you know. He would put you to work in an instant if you needed the job. Having so many lose their source of income? No. That's not Mike."

"You're right. Just, it sucks. You know? Anyways, girl in the back? I vaguely remember her. Teri told her when she was seated I wouldn't serve her back there by her lonesome. She said that was fine and got up to get her own drink."

"So you never served her? Not even once?"

"No. Why?"

"She said—" Skye was interrupted before finishing the sentence.

"She? You have talked to her?"

"Yes. I have." No need for him to tell Monique that Kendall was staying with him. He really didn't need the headache. "Anyways, she said that when she returned from the stage, there was a second glass of wine waiting for her at the table. We wondered where it came from. Who bought it for her?"

"Gee, sexy. I can't tell you. It wasn't me. Figured I wouldn't get tipped, sitting by herself. And as you know, it was pretty full last night with drunken party girls who never know what they are forking over when they are smashed."

"You didn't see anyone else at the bar getting drinks?"

"Wasn't paying attention. If I was on the floor, which I was every time you were dancing, then I was focused on you and getting drinks to the right people."

Skye frowned. "Alright. Thanks for your time."

"Wait."

"What?"

"Can I see you soon? We can still go out for drinks or dinner. Hell, I will even cook dinner. Just come over?"

"I can't right now. Thanks for the invite. I'll talk to you later."

Quickly, he disconnected the call. The only other one who might know would be Nick, the bartender. It took him a couple of minutes to look through his contact list, but he remembered after a bit he filed him under B for bartender not N for Nick. When he first got Nick's number he didn't quite remember his name, so it was the more logical choice and he just never changed it. Securing the number, he pushed the little green phone symbol to make the call.

"Hello?"

"Hey, Nick? It's Skye."

"Hey, dude. What's up?"

"Need to pick your brain about last night's service."

"What about it?"

"Do you remember a girl getting her own glass of wine before the show?"

"Yeah."

"When she was on stage, her glass was refilled. Do you remember who might have got it?"

It was quiet on the line for a moment.

"Nick? You still there?"

"Yeah, was thinking."

"Well, next time breathe heavy or something so I know the line didn't go dead."

Nick snorts. "You should be so lucky. I don't remember pouring out any more wine that evening. The drunk chicks in the front were all drinking shots or mixers. A couple of sodas, designated drivers most likely, but that's about it. She was the only one I remember serving wine to and it was just the one glass. Why?"

Skye frowned deeply, rubbing his forehead in thought. "She had a second glass waiting for her when she came back from the stage. We just can't figure out how she got it."

"Well, if Mike thinks I'm stealing to give away product, then he can shove it up his ass."

"No, no. Mike doesn't think that. I'm sure that the cost of a glass of wine is the least of his concerns right now."

"True that. So, what's the beef about then?"

"Nothing, man. Just trying to solve a mystery, is all."

"Dude, you are not making sense. What diff does it make if she got a second glass of wine or not?"

"Because someone has tried to kill her twice, and I'm wondering if it might actually have been three times."

"Are you accusing me of, what? Poisoning her or something?"

"No, Nick. Not at all. Trying to find out how she might have gotten the drink. Who bought it? How did it end up on her table? Monique says she didn't bring it to her. You say you didn't pour it. So, where did it come from? It's just a bit strange."

"Yeah. It is, but I didn't pour it, so I don't know what to tell you."

"Thanks, dude. Appreciate it."

"No need to thank me. I didn't do anything."

"No, but you did eliminate another possibility and, even though it still leaves the mystery, at least it doesn't leave us wondering."

"Us? You with the chick now? Did you do her?"

"None of your fucking business."

"So, no. Damn. Didn't think she would turn you down. Or she that ugly you couldn't get it up?"

"Shit, Nick. Get your mind out of the gutter. She is beautiful and very nice. It's just been crazy with everything the past day." Not that Skye didn't want to have sex with her. But he wasn't going to push her, and he didn't want it to just be a one-night stand. Nick didn't need to know this, though. Besides, he still thought she might like other women more. Figures. The one woman who caught his interest couldn't care less about him because he was a man.

"Just saying, with a female to turn your good looks down, something ain't right."

"Just saying, it's not your fucking business. Thanks for the info, Nick. I'll talk to you later."

"Yeah. No problem."

Skye hung up, aggravated by Nick and the lack of putting an end to the extra drink mystery. Feeling a presence behind him, he turned to see Kendall standing by the door. "You find everything okay?"

"Yes. Thank you." She heard just the tail end of his phone conversation and wasn't exactly sure what it was about, but it seemed to have annoyed him. As a result, she hesitated about interrupting him.

"Did you need something?"

"No. I… I just thought…" She looked abashed, contrite. She realized she probably should have stayed in the room he had assigned her.

"Thought what?"

"Nothing. Sorry I disturbed you." Kendall turned to head back upstairs.

Skye scrubbed his face with his hand for a moment, then let his hand push back his hair. With just a couple of purposeful steps, he was behind her and grabbed her arm to stop her retreat.

"Sorry. You didn't disturb me. I was actually talking to Nick, the bartender at the club last night, and he gets under my skin every now and again. Don't go. Come back in the kitchen. I was just about to make some coffee. Would you like some?"

When Skye stopped her with his hand on her arm, she suddenly found him very close to her. Those eyes! Good god, they were piercing and vibrant. They made her heart flutter. If only he knew what he did to her insides when he was this close, she was positive he would run screaming for the hills just to get away. Every fiber in her being was instantly heated, her blood flowing through her veins like molten lava.

He let go of her arm, taking a step back. "Please? I have a few things we need to talk about."

Business. Yes. She could deal with business and not think about being a fool under that mindful gaze of his. "Sure."

Skye turned back to the kitchen and offered her a variety of choices for the Keurig machine. She selected a dark roast while he filled the machine with water and grabbed a mug to put under it. He took another cup out for himself for when hers was done.

"First, did you come down for anything in particular? Is Tinkerbell all settled in?"

"Nothing in particular. Tinkerbell is still checking out the place. New territory for her and she is very skittish after this morning's events. She must have been terrified when the fire started. Between that and the new place and all the new smells, she is still nervous. She is hiding under the bed, and it's best to let her adjust on her own." She shuffled her feet a bit before she continued, "I can't thank you enough. Saving her, saving *me*. Letting us stay here, stopping to get things for both of us. I will pay you back. I swear."

"Not worried about it, Kendall. Get on your feet, first, and worry about paying me back later, or never. Whichever."

"No. I insist on paying you back. It's just going to take a while."

Skye grabbed her mug and put it down in front of her. "If you want cream or sugar, they are already on the table."

"Thanks." Kendall had more than enough. She sat down in front of the coffee mug and buried her face in her hands. She didn't want to be weak in front of him. She didn't like showing vulnerability. She was the strong one, proud and determined, but even this was too much for her.

Skye started his own coffee brewing, but when he turned back to Kendall, his heart twisted. She appeared so small and lost. He moved towards her, squatting beside her chair. Skye put a hand on her shoulder, the other around her front, encircling her within his arms, and tilted her towards him.

"You're welcome, baby. It's going to be okay. You'll see."

She moved her hands away from her face, glancing over at him. "You're so kind. You don't need to be dealing with a distraught female you don't even know."

He squeezed her tight, then released her as he stood and moved to the side chair, pulling it closer to her but not touching her. She seemed uncomfortable with his physical contact. "If you weren't a bit upset, I would think you might be a robot. Hell, Kendall, you've been through so much as it is. I know you're still getting over your mother's death. Now, with everything that has been going on in the past sixteen hours, it's pretty intense. I think you are handling it with far more aplomb and poise than most would in this situation."

Kendall shrugged and moved the coffee mug closer, keeping her hands around it. "I've always been one to deal with the issues first and break down in private later. I had to. Mom was sick for a long time and it was just the prudent course to take. Although, I admit, I am finding a lot of this hard to grasp or accept."

"I know. I am finding it a bit difficult to, as well." Skye got up to get his fresh-brewed coffee and returned carrying his own mug to sit beside her again. He rested one hand on her wrist. "I'll help you through this. I won't let anything happen to you."

"Again, you have been so kind and words are just not enough to say thank you."

"Don't worry about it. I'm glad to help." He pulled his hand away somewhat reluctantly. "While you were upstairs, I made a couple of phone calls. I'm afraid the mysteries still persist."

"What do you mean?"

Before he could respond, his phone rang and he moved to pick it up.

"Hello?"

"Mr. Falcon?"

"Speaking."

"Officer Charles, here. Is Ms. Roberts still with you?"

"Yes, sir. Is something wrong?"

"Actually, yes. Ms. Roberts' vehicle exploded about fifteen minutes ago. The explosion also set fire to three more vehicles nearby."

Skye growled. "Are you fucking kidding me?"

His angry outburst startled Kendall, who looked at him with deep concern. She knew it was something else about her, in some form or other, and whatever it was, it was not good news.

"No, Mr. Falcon. I am not. I'll need her to come down to impound to assess the damage. She will also need to contact her insurance company again."

"I don't think she has called them about the house yet. It's been a crazy day, as it is. Fine. How soon?"

"Preferably as soon as possible."

"Okay. Should I let the squad outside know we are leaving or what?"

"No, sir. I will take care of that. We will still want them to keep surveillance on the property while you are both away."

"Fine. See you in about a half hour." Skye hung up the phone and turned to Kendall, unsure how to tell her. She already knew something was up from listening to his side of the call.

"What happened now?"

"We need to go to the impound lot. Seems your car just exploded and damaged three other vehicles."

"Are you kidding me?" she asked aghast.

"Sadly, I wish I were. No. I told him I'd have you there in the next 30 minutes or so."

"I can't believe this. What next? What is left? My life is totally gone. All I have left is Tinkerbell. This can't be happening! This can't be real!"

Skye moved to her side and pulled her up into his arms, encasing her tightly. He rocked her gently as he tried to give her some comfort. "I know, baby. I know. Tinkerbell is safe and we can work on everything else together. I'll help you."

He called her baby again. He offered her help and guidance, support and to be with her. But, she didn't trust him. Surely it couldn't just be for the sake of getting in her pants anymore. So what? Pity? That was just as bad. She pushed him back. "You're in danger, too. Because of me and whatever reason this guy is after me."

"So what? Are you just going to walk out that door and take your chances with whoever is out there gunning for you?"

"No. Yes? No. Shit. I don't know. I..." She gave in to his embrace then, leaning her head against his beating heart. "I don't know what to do. I don't know how to fix this. Or how to make it go away. I'm not able to see any solution when I can't fully see the problem."

Skye held her close and kissed the top of her head. He probably shouldn't have, but he couldn't help himself. She touched a part of him he didn't think possible. When she tilted her head up to him, surprised at the gentle caress of his lips upon her head, he cupped her cheek and stared into her eyes.

Slowly, he leaned down and kissed her softly. His lips took hers without demands, without pressure. He wasn't even sure she wouldn't slap him when he pulled back. However, he was too enchanted with her to care.

All his life, he had been alone. He was fine with it, overall. But if he were truthful, he would admit that he would be jealous of those couples in the park or at the store, walking hand in hand and being truly in love. Especially those older couples who had been together for decades. They were so comfortable with each other, and yet, still so much in love. He wanted that for himself. Someone whom he could care about and who would love him regardless. A woman who would stand by his side through thick and thin. A woman who wanted him for who he truly was, not for his good looks. In time those would fade, but his heart would remain the same. And most of all, he wanted a woman he could trust to go through life with him, not use him or go behind his back whenever she got bored with him.

He saw those qualities in Kendall. A woman of

substance. A woman whose heart was pure and loving. She was a person who seemed loyal and honest. Even the little time he had spent with her gave him that impression. He backed away from her lips, his thumb still on her cheek and caressing her soft skin. "I'm sorry. I know I shouldn't have done that."

Kendall frowned and backed up out of his reach. She was a fool. She let him in, got lost in those eyes and succumbed to his kiss. She should have known better. She ought to have realized he only kissed her to calm her down. "It's fine." She spun on her heel and headed towards the garage.

"You said we needed to go to the impound lot?" She needed to compose herself. Walking and focusing on what needed to be done helped her.

Skye scrubbed his face. *Way to go, asshole,* he chided himself. She didn't want him, wasn't interested in him. She made that perfectly clear. Repeatedly. Yet, with each no, he wanted her more. Why? Was it because she didn't fawn over him, because she was hard to attain, impossible to get?

Was it the challenge that intrigued him after all? He honestly didn't have the answer to any of those questions.

"Yeah. We do. I also had a few other things I wanted to you talk about as well. I can do that while I drive. Tinkerbell going to be okay?"

"As long as the house doesn't catch fire, she should be fine."

"Please. Don't say that even in jest. Not with everything going on now."

"You're right. Sorry. That was in extremely poor taste. I'm usually not so glib."

"I've a feeling neither of us are at our best in these current circumstances."

Skye held the cab door open for her. Once she was settled, he went around to the driver's side and climbed in.

As they drove, he told her about the calls he had made. "The fact that no one knows where that drink came from concerns me."

"Why? I mean, it was just a drink. What difference would it make who brought it to the table or bought it?"

He gave her an incredulous look. "Because it's not normal. Plus, you said it made you feel lightheaded and dizzy."

"Probably because I drank the second one so fast."

"Do you really think that's it? Listen. I wish I could say it was just something innocent, like you being a bit intoxicated, but with that on top of everything else, it just doesn't jive right. As part of the POC for the fire department, we're also trained with some basic EMT skills. I admit I put it off to being slightly drunk, too, until everything else happened and the fact no one brought you that drink. Just makes me suspicious enough to think the drink might have been drugged."

"With what?"

"A number of things. Uppers? Downers? There are several drugs out there that can slow down your reflexes. In a high enough dosage, could have even caused your heart to stop."

"And of course, there would be no evidence of

it now."

"Actually that's not true. Drugs can be found within a system two to four days after it was taken. A standard ten-point drug screening test can show everything, including prescription drugs such as oxycodone, barbiturates, benzodiazepines, ecstasy, other illegal drugs, and even how much alcohol you consumed. It's been less than 24 hours, so whatever you had, even if it was just plain wine, will show up. I, personally, would just feel better knowing that is one less thing we have to be concerned with." He glanced at her sideways for a brief moment before turning back to the road. "It's your choice, of course. Your decision. But if you want, I have some buddies at the lab and we can get the test done."

Kendall stared out the window for a few moments contemplating everything he had told her. As they pulled up to the impound lot, she was well aware of the chaos still going on in the center. What was left of her smoldering car was visible at the center of the pandemonium. There were several fire trucks, police cars and various onlookers crowded around the inside and outside of the impound lot. So many, no one noticed the black Corvette just a few doors down with blackened windows.

Chapter Eleven

By the time Skye pulled into the garage for his place, he knew Kendall was exhausted both physically and emotionally, and he couldn't blame her one bit.

After the impound lot and filling out all the paperwork, they headed over to the insurance company. Kendall filled out the tons of forms there, as well. Then off to the DMV to get a new driver's license. Next to the bank to check her finances and set up some checks so she could pay some bills. Finally, the mall for a new phone, some clothes, and a few other miscellaneous things she was going to need while she stayed at Skye's.

"I'll get your bags. Go inside. You still have some phone calls to make to your credit card companies and stuff. While you're doing that, I am going to make us some dinner. Do you realize, outside of breakfast, neither of us has had anything to eat?"

"No, I hadn't. I'm not sure I have much of an appetite with everything happening today."

"I get it, but we both need to keep up our strength. I'll bring these bags upstairs for you. Go on in."

Kendall got out of the truck and headed into the house. She headed up to her room and found Tinkerbell sitting on top of the bed. She looked a bit calmer and stood when Kendall entered. Keeping the door open, Kendall sat next to her beloved pet, scooping her up in her arms to hold and pet her.

Moments later, Skye was there with an armful of bags. He set them just inside the door.

"How is she doing?"

"She seems a bit more relaxed than she was when we first got here. I think she realizes it's a safe place. She is not one for a lot of noise or activity, so being alone probably helped her after her experience this morning."

"May I?" He held his hand out, indicating he wanted to pet Tinkerbell.

Setting Tinkerbell alongside of her on the bed,

she nodded. Walking over to them, Skye kept his hand out to let Tinkerbell sniff it, squatting to bring him more to her level on the bed. She then rubbed her face against it. "She seems to like you. She doesn't always like others, at least not right away."

"She might remember I was the one who got her out of a burning building and handed her back to you."

"You might be right. She is pretty intelligent. Obviously a good judge of character."

Skye chuckled as he scratched Tinkerbell's ears. After a few minutes, he stood up. "I'm going to go get dinner started. You have a few phone calls I know you still need to make. If you need anything in the meantime, just holler." When he reached the door, he stood there with his hand on the knob. "Open or closed?"

"Closed, please. I am not quite ready for this curious little girl to go traipsing about just yet."

He nodded and shut the door.

The black Corvette hung back as it followed the GMC Sierra 1500 around the town. Thank goodness he was a very patient person, because this was getting annoying. He was all over the place following them. After a long day of gallivanting about, he finally followed them to a home. The address hadn't come up for the GMC, so he was a bit confused as to how the owner kept it off the net. Not that he cared. His goal was more about who was currently inside. Why did she have to be there last night? Why did she have to see him? Or at least, he thought she did. Regardless, he couldn't take the chance.

Now that he knew where they were going to be, Zebart Holiday moved off. He had a few more supplies to obtain before he could put an end to this part of his mission and move on.

As the Corvette drove off, Zebart glanced up at his visor. There was a picture of his beautiful daughter, full of life, a smile as big as the outdoors. He reached up and touched the picture. He wished he could give his own life in exchange to bring her back. It was all he wanted. All he desired. However, he would protect others like her. He would make sure this world was cleaned of the horny filth that walked it. It would take him a multitude of years to accomplish his goal, but he was of one mind, one purpose. He would succeed because he had to. He couldn't save his daughter, but he would save the daughters of many others. He would make sure they would be okay and no other father would have to suffer as he did.

Chapter Twelve

Barney opened up his email and noticed he had one from the state lab center. Eagerly, he opened it up. *Took them long enough,* he thought as he started to process what he was reading, bypassing the generalities of the report at the beginning. It was all pretty much all the same; who did the analyses, the date and time they were done, who signed off on it, etc. What he needed to see were the results and summations made by the scientists. Finally reaching that part of the email, he brought a notepad and pen to his side just in case he had any questions or concerns he would need to respond to. Once he accomplished that, he began to read, his frown, then scowl increasing as he continued.

Chemical Analysis of explosion site:
0.15 Nitric Acid
0.15 Ammonia
0.15 Chlorine

0.15 Sulfuric Acid
0.10 Grain Alcohol
0.05 Water

Trace elements of the following: Platinum, palladium, carbon, hydrogen, copper, tin, zinc, sulfur, fluorine, phosphorous, and silicon.

Results of analysis: a chemical explosive detonated by a cell phone resulted in the burn patterns distributed in such a way as to be highly combustible. All the chemicals to make the explosive device can be obtained by ordinary household, automobile and pool products. When mixed together, these chemicals became highly unstable, resulting in an ebullient, volatile material that erupted to an unstable combination of incendiary force.

No DNA or clear fingerprints were denoted on the remaining pieces examined from the blast zone. A partial fingerprint has been sent along with the report for analysis by the appropriate database.

Please note: this file has been red flagged.

Please read below for additional results.

Barney dropped his pen to the floor as he continued to read the additional notes made on the file, including a possible lead on the partial print. Scrubbing his face with both hands, he swung around in his chair. He needed a few moments before he continued with this knowledge. It would be the second one in his lifetime and the idea turned his stomach.

As a fire investigator, it was required they recertify every four years. Even still, most people take additional courses on a yearly basis in order to become acquainted with new ways being developed in detecting an arsonist.

Barney's first experience with a serial arsonist was in California, where he had attended an arson investigators convention. Coincidentally, during the convention, several fires broke out around the city. By doing research, they noticed at the same time the conventions were being held, several fires occurred around the city. The convention center fell within the center of the outbreak of burning buildings each and every time. They also determined the sites of the blazes were connected by major highways easily accessible by the exits. It seemed logical to conclude the arsonist would have hopped off the exit, started the fire, then moved to start the next one. The deciding factor was that there were two other fire investigator conventions that had identical incidents during the conventions held within their cities with hundreds of fires and millions of dollars in damages.

A fingerprint left at the first set of fires was found on a time-delayed incendiary device. However, fingerprint technology was not as advanced in 1985 and the evidence was basically useless. By the time of the third convention in 1992 and the subsequent series of events, the investigators were able to pinpoint the fingerprint to one man. The man was a volunteer firefighter who was known for his heroism by calling in fires within his hometown before others could sound the alarm or, in some cases, forcefully declare a particular fire was arson and not a random electrical fire started by accident.

Over the years, as well as with the aforementioned case, Barney learned volunteer or POC firemen are usually the primary model for firefighters who turn to arson because there is less scrutiny when they are hired on. As a result, these types of arsonists will set the fire and then become the hero by reporting it, evacuating the building or both, and then watch from the sidelines for excitement. They are even willing to join the fray and become part of the activity by entering the fire, even for the pure excitement of it. It has been determined these arsonists are psychopaths who get a thrill from the inadvertent attention by experiencing a fire they created.

So, who was on the scene each time a fire occurred? Who was quick to jump in the fray? And who was a POC for the Moraine Valley Fire Department? Who fit the profile of a psychopath: loner, cold-hearted planner, and one who calculates every move? Who has been the savior of the day, thereby gaining the hero status? And who has been calling and asking for updates on the case to make sure he wasn't found out or left any evidence behind? And who matched the partial? Skye Falcon.

Barney picked up the phone and, for the first time in his career, he dialed a number he really didn't want to.

Chapter Thirteen

Days had gone by, and Kendall was settling in nicely within Skye's home. She told him a couple of times she should start looking for an apartment, but he reminded her she was still being hunted by someone and it wasn't safe. Part of him didn't want to let her go. Having her in his home meant he got to know about her better, which made it harder and harder to think there would soon come a day when nothing he said would stop her from leaving.

Skye was still pretty positive she was only interested in women, and the more they spent time together, the more he was sure of it. She continually stayed a respectful distance from him. Except for that one-time kiss and hug, she didn't really let him get physically close. She was very good at keeping him at arm's length and figured it was because she didn't want to hurt his feelings after everything he was doing for her. Yet, the more he got to know her, the more he realized she was the kind of woman he wanted, with only one major flaw. She didn't want him. It was a circumstance he was totally unfamiliar with, and he was unsure how to deal with it. So he continued to think of her strictly as a friend and bury the rising additional feelings he was having.

At least the last few days have been quiet. No additional fires, no further attempts on her life. Admittedly, there was still an unmarked squad car outside, and because of his current circumstances, he hadn't been called to help with even a small local blaze. Even Tinkerbell was adjusting nicely to the quiet surroundings of her new home. Albeit, Kendall insisted it would only be temporary.

Skye knocked on her door.

"Come in."

"Hey. Dinner is almost ready."

"I thought I was going to cook tonight."

Skye chuckled. "Yeah, well, I got hungry."

"I'm sorry. I lost track of time. I'll clean up."

Skye shuffled his feet slightly, unmoving from the doorframe.

Kendall gave him a curious look, her eyes

furrowing in concern.

"Was there something else?"

"Yeah. Actually, I got a phone call from Michael."

"Michael? The club owner?"

"Yeah. Anyways, he says that he heard from the insurance company and he can start rebuilding in about three weeks. He has to give the guys time to finish investigating before he gets the money to start rebuilding."

"Oh. That's good. Raul, you and the other guys will be back to work in no time."

Thing was, Skye didn't want to go back to dancing. He did it for a decent income, for something to do and because it was a chance to meet some women. What he hadn't realized before now was he wasn't interested in the women he met there, at least with the exception of Kendall, and she wasn't interested in him. All the other women he had met there were so superficial, or taken, or not really his taste. Kendall was so different. The moment he saw her, he could tell. Now that he had gotten to know her better, he was more sure than ever before. Finding someone else like her was going to be difficult, if not entirely impossible. He certainly didn't need the money, but she was not aware of it and he preferred it stay that way.

"Yeah. Although Raul and some of the others might have to find other jobs to tide them over in the meantime."

"Of course. You have the fire department to bring in extra money. Is that what you wanted to talk about? Of course, silly me. I've been so wrapped up in my own issues I hadn't even thought about offering you rent or something for while I am here."

Kendall stood and moved closer to the door to retrieve her checkbook. "How much did you want?"

"Shit. No, Kendall. That's not what I was referring to at all. You are my guest here. I don't want your money." Did she really think he was that shallow?

Kendall turned around with a frown. "I'm sorry. I didn't mean to insult you. I thought. Never mind. I'm glad the club will get rebuilt and you can all go back to work in time." She stopped and lifted her nose, sniffing, concern lacing her next words. "Do you smell something burning?"

Skye inhaled deeply. He ran to the stairs. "Fuck me. The kitchen is on fire."

"What!" Kendall ran towards the staircase on Skye's heels as he took the stairs two and three at a time.

"Stay back! I got this." He grabbed a fire extinguisher from the pantry and used it on the stove, which was engulfed in flames. Once it was out, Skye leaned against sink and started to laugh.

Kendall watched him, stunned at his reaction. When he finally calmed down enough, he turned to her as he pointed to the stove. "I think I just destroyed dinner. Guess we are going to have to order a pizza or something."

"Can we do that? I mean with the squad there and all?"

"It's pizza. I'm not dialing 1-800-bomb-me-2."

"Then let me pay for it, at least."

"No way. I burned dinner, and I'm sure I destroyed my stove in the process. I'll pay for the pizza. Is there anywhere in particular you like?"

"No. I don't live on this side of town, so I am not sure what there is. Whatever you get is fine."

"What do you like on your pizza?"

"I'm good with anything but onions, anchovies and green peppers."

"That's great. Those are not my favorites, either. Cheese and sausage okay, then?"

"Classic. Sure, that's fine."

Skye ordered the pizza, then called the station so they could radio the unmarked car about the delivery. An hour later, the pizza was delivered. Skye answered the door and paid for the pie, then carried it into the kitchen where Kendall already had plates out. "I should have let you answer the door. The delivery person was a really pretty female."

"Did she scare you or something? Make a pass?"

Skye gave her a quizzical look as he laughed.

"No. I just thought she might be more your type."

Kendall stopped what she was doing and gave him a totally astonished look. "You think I am a lesbian?"

For the first time in he couldn't remember how long, he was actually embarrassed. "Yes? I mean, I don't care if you are. It doesn't bother me or anything. But, yes."

She stood upright in shock. "Wow. I had no idea I came across that way. I'm not, by the way. I'm glad it doesn't bother you if I were, but I'm not. Or. Wait. Are you uncomfortable with me being here, knowing now I lean towards liking men?"

"No. That's not what I meant at all." Realizing he opened up a major can of shitass suck worms, he inhaled deeply and spoke honestly. "You just kept your distance from me after that one time we kissed. I figured you didn't like it because you didn't like men. I didn't realize it was just me you didn't care for."

Weak in the knees, Kendall plopped onto the kitchen chair, her eyes never leaving those oceans of turquoise blue. "That's not it at all. I'm sorry I made you feel that way. I just didn't want to get close to you. I didn't want to take the chance."

Skye sat down, opening up the pizza box and setting it between the two of them. He doubted it would get touched much until this conversation was over with, but he felt she would want something else to focus on, even for just a moment or two, and the pizza seemed to be the logical distraction. "Take what chance?"

She reached for a slice of pizza and put it on the plate in front of her. "Listen. I know I am not beautiful. I know I don't turn men's heads. And you? You're very handsome. You can have any woman in the world. How can I ever even consider competing against that? I didn't. I don't want a one-night stand, which was all I felt I would have gotten that first night. Since fate has thrown us together, I didn't want to take advantage of your hospitality, and I also didn't want to start something that was going to end when it was safe again. I would then be going back to my own world. I didn't think I could do that, if I gave in."

Skye had no reply for her. Sure, he could tell her how wrong she was. How it didn't have to be that way. How he was interested in more than just bedding her for a couple of nights. But why would she have any cause to believe him? Truth was, he wasn't even sure himself if he only wanted her because she hadn't been interested. Now that he knew somewhat differently, how did it change his perception, if at all? "Forgive me. I shouldn't have assumed and made you feel uncomfortable. Please. Let's forget this conversation ever occurred and enjoy the pizza before it gets too cold."

Skye focused on his food, though his mind was millions of miles away, and yet also sitting right across the table from him. He knew she was emotionally strong, getting through the past couple of days with nary a complaint told him volumes about her personality. Her calm demeanor in the face of disaster let him know even more about her and he was impressed with all of it. Yet, her latest confession enlightened something he had never realized until now. She was scared of opening her heart. It was easier for her to keep everyone at arm's length in order to protect herself from being hurt. Although Skye knew about her parents and lack of siblings, he wondered if there was some other past boyfriend who abandoned her, too, for her to be so emotionally delicate, or if it was just the loss of her mother that affected her outlook so. He realized he better be sure in what he wanted before he did anything. He certainly didn't need to hurt her because of his not being genuine in regards to his own desires.

A pounding on his door broke his reverie and made Kendall jump. They exchanged worried looks before Skye got up to answer the door. Kendall followed him, but stayed back, just in case.

Skye unlocked the deadbolts and peeked through a crack in the door before opening it wider.

"Hi, Barney. Officer Charles." At first he smiled in welcome, but then he saw additional officers behind the two and the serious looks on their faces. "What's going on?"

"Sorry, Skye." Barney stepped back, allowing the other officers to rush past him and push Skye against the wall.

Brett came in behind them. "Skye Falcon? You are under arrest for arson."

Chapter Fourteen

Kendall gasped, bracing herself against the door jamb she was standing by. Her eyes wide with fearful disbelief as Skye struggled against the police who were in the process of cuffing his wrists behind his back.

"Are you fucking nuts? I've been with Kendall the entire time. I'm a fucking fireman myself!"

Barney moved over to Skye. "The chem report came back. Among everything, they found a partial print on the detonator. We have a warrant to search your house. With a detonator, Ms. Roberts can be the perfect alibi."

"It's not safe. Not for her. I couldn't be driving the car that was trying to kill her. Please. Her life is still at risk! Please. Don't leave her alone. It's not safe. It's not safe." Skye kept calling out as the police pulled him out of the house and into the awaiting car. His cries were cut off as the car door shut.

Brett moved over to Kendall. "Ma'am, we would like you to come with us. For your safety and to ask you a few questions."

"Tinkerbell?"

"Excuse me?"

"My cat. Upstairs. Going through the house will terrify her and she is already skittish since the fire at my place."

"Of course. Do you have a carrier for her? You can bring her with."

"Yes. I do." It took Kendall a few moments to regain her composure enough to go upstairs to her room and get the carrier and Tinkerbell while an officer accompanied her. When she was ready, they led her out of the house and to another waiting car to drive her to the police station.

Barney and Brett stayed at the house while four other officers began searching for evidence of Skye having set the fires.

One officer called from the basement, "You better come down here and see this."

Barney and Brett both headed down the stairs.

In the center of the main room was a huge work table with incriminating items on it. Five partially dismantled cell phones, a bottle of Ethyl Rubbing Alcohol, a bottle of Hydrogen Peroxide, a bottle of nail polish remover with acetone, as well as several tools scattered about. Barney and Brett exchanged looks, Barney frowning all the more. He had really hoped the partial was a mistake.

Another officer called from the top of the stairs, "We found a couple of the items you were looking for in the garage."

"Coming," Brett responded as he and Barney headed to the area.

In the garage, a couple of old batteries, one for an automobile and one for a boat, were found. Both would contain sulfuric acid. On the other side of the garage were some old bottles of pool cleaners, of which chlorine was the major ingredient. Rubbing the back of his neck, Barney grumbled, "I want to be in on the interrogation, if you don't mind."

Brett shook his head. "I understand. I can't let you in the interrogation room, but you can be in the observation room behind it."

"That's fine. I can't believe this. I just can't believe Skye is the perp."

"That's the thing about psychopaths, Barn. You know this as well as I. Unlike sociopaths, they are good at blending in and looking normal."

"This fucking sucks. I hope you know that." Barney headed out to his truck. They had all the evidence they needed to start questioning. It was being bagged and tagged by the other officers.

Meanwhile, Kendall sat in an interrogation room with Tinkerbell on her lap. None of this seemed real. None of this could actually be happening, could it? Things like this don't happen to boring people like her.

Her hand ran through the soft fur of Tinkerbell. A part of her was glad she didn't sleep with Skye. *Shit! Can you imagine if you gave in to that body? To a brief moment of desire with a man so crazed with power he burned up his place of employment? Or my house? Or my car? Is that why he set his sights on me at the club? So he would have an excuse to destroy what I still have left of my pitiful life? I must have looked so pathetic he saw a world-class sucker and he had to pick me out of the multitudes of women at the club that night. Such a freaking fool I am. Such a screwed up, freaking fool. I was beginning to believe I was something more to him than convenient.*

Chapter Fifteen

Officer Brett Charles entered the interrogation room and sat across from Skye. Opening a folder, he took a few moments to read it before he acknowledged Skye's presence.

"Just to clarify, you have been read your rights?"

"Yes."

"Do you understand them as they were read to you?"

"Yes."

"Do you have anything to say?"

"I didn't do it."

"Doesn't everyone say that?"

"Probably. In my case it's true. You will see."

"You don't want a lawyer, Mr. Falcon?"

"No. I don't need one. I am innocent."

"Actually, I would recommend one."

Skye sat stoically, waiting. Brett pulled some photos from the file he had on the table in front of him. They were of the workshop downstairs and of the chemicals in Skye's garage.

"Would you care to explain all of this?"

Skye pulled the photos close to him to see what they were, then tossed them back onto the table and looked into Brett's eyes, unblinking. "That's my worktable in the basement. I get some damaged or old cell phones and I try and clean them up with the hydrogen peroxide. I use the acetone and the rubbing alcohol for cleaning different parts. The acetone also acts as a base for getting some of the silicon in the phones to be non-corrosive. I fiddle with them to see if I can get them working again. Those I manage to get working, I donate to the American Legion to use for our servicemen overseas. They collect those, you know."

"And the batteries? The pool supplies?"

"Those are actually extra batteries that were in my parents' garage before they passed. I keep waiting for a village recycling day to dispose of them properly, but I keep forgetting when that day occurs. As for the pool supplies. Same thing. My parents had a pool. When I had to clean out what was left of the garage after the fire, that stuff was just quickly packed and I have not had a chance to get rid of it properly. Why? Oh. Wait. Fuck me. Those are the chemicals found in the analysis by the state labs?"

"Yes. Combined together, and with a cell phone detonator, they are the remnants of what was uncovered at the club's blast point of origin. Along with a partial print that you match."

"A partial means you only confirmed a few lines or swirls and could be a match for anyone. Listen. It wasn't me. I didn't do this. I'm not the person who enjoys watching things burn or in it for the glory of being some kind of perverse hero. However, I am worried about Kendall. Is she still at the house? Is she still under protection? Someone tried to kill her. She is not safe by herself."

"Currently, Ms. Roberts is here at the station. We have a few questions for her, as well. We can drive her back to wherever she would like to stay when we are through with her."

"Can I have my phone call then? You can't just send her out there by herself."

"You can have your phone call in a couple of minutes. I want to talk to you about something else, first."

"And that would be?"

Brett shuffled through the folder until he found what he was looking for. "Your arrest record."

Skye was quiet a few moments, almost growling as he realized where this line of interrogation was going. "I was released and charges dropped."

"Only for lack of evidence."

"Only because there was no evidence to find. I didn't start the fire that killed my parents."

"Yet, you were the only one who survived."

"Brett. Do you honestly think that doesn't haunt me every day of my life?"

"Your psychiatric evaluation states you were pretty cold and manipulative. According to the doctor's report, you fit the profile of someone who is cold and intelligent, mimicking what others do.

You tell them what you think they want to hear, what they hope to hear, while secretly enjoying the chaos that you brought."

"It says all that?"

"That and more. According to this report, you weren't home when the fire started, but since you were only seventeen and it was at two in the morning, one has to wonder why you weren't where you should have been."

"Then you should also read in the report I told them I snuck out to go to a friend's house for a party."

Officer Charles looked over a few more sheets of paper, stopping to read one of them. "Ah, yes you did. However, your friend, Dustin Mallow, stated he didn't remember seeing you after one. That doesn't cover the hour before the fire started."

"That's because I was with his sister and he didn't know. He was very protective of his sister."

"And this wasn't brought up back then because?"

"Because it wasn't needed. I had just lost my

house and my parents. The fire department declared it an electrical fire that started from faulty wiring. Why the fuck would you think I would kill my parents?"

"So you could be the hero. Just like you were for Ms. Roberts."

"In case this has escaped you, I wasn't the hero for my parents. They died in that fire. What happened with my folks only gave me incentive to become a fireman in order to try and help others from losing their family or their house. As for Ms. Roberts, what I did for her had nothing to do with her being rescued from fires, but from a madman who is trying to kill her. Now, those charges were dropped for a reason. I didn't kill my parents. I would never want anyone, especially my family, to have been hurt like that. Furthermore, I would like my phone call without any further delay."

Brett pulled out his phone and slid it over to Skye. "Make your call. I'll step out for a few moments to give you some privacy."

Skye nodded, picked up Officer Charles' phone

and dialed the only one he could think of. Thank goodness it was also a number he knew by heart and not by the number on a speed dial. He figured the investigator gave him his cell phone to trace the call, listen in on the call or even to get a better print, but he didn't care. Kendall's life was more important at the moment and, overall, he was innocent.

"Hello?"

"Raul! Dude. I need a major favor."

"Skye? Didn't I already give you one? You and your girl stayed here?"

"Yeah. And I truly appreciate that, but that's why I am calling. I need another one."

"Man, you owe me big. What do you need now?"

"Look. I've been arrested."

"What?!"

"Yeah. Long story short, they think I am the one who set fire to the club."

"Did you?"

"Fuck! You know me better than that! I can't

believe you had to ask. No. I didn't start it."

"Okay. Okay. Chill, dude. I was just checking. So what do you need? Bail? Lawyer? What?"

"I need you to come by the station and get Kendall. They have her here, too, for questioning, but someone is still after her and she needs to be safe. Please? Come pick her up and stay with her until I get out? I need to know she is going to be okay. I can deal with everything else, but not if I have to worry about her being killed by the lunatic who is trying to off her."

"Yeah. I can do that. I'll be at the station in an hour. Let her know I am coming?"

"I'll try and get word to her. I'm hoping Officer Charles will at least be kind enough to tell her for me. Thanks, man. I really owe you."

"Don't worry, dude. You'll pay."

Chapter Sixteen

Officer Charles entered the room where Kendall was still sitting with Tinkerbell laying on the table. She looked up at him as he entered, her hand buried in the fur of her companion.

"What is going on?"

Brett sat down with a file in front of him, but didn't say anything just yet.

"Am I in trouble or something?"

"Should you be?"

"No. I haven't done anything wrong."

"Then I guess you have nothing to worry about."

"So, what's going on?" Kendall repeated nervously.

"I need to ask you some questions, if you don't mind."

"No. I don't mind. Anything to help."

"How long have you known Skye?"

"Just a couple of days. I met him last Friday at

the club. Same night I met you, remember?"

"When he walked you out of the building, how did he appear?"

"What do you mean?"

"Was he nervous? Anxious?"

"No. He seemed a bit, I don't know. Disappointed? I had told him goodnight and I was leaving without any further ado. I think he was kind of surprised I didn't want to be with him more."

"Be with him? Can you explain?"

"Well, he brought me up on stage, then asked if I'd stay behind until he met me after the show. I hadn't planned to, but the second glass of wine I had kind of threw me for a loop. I seem to have lost track of time and the next thing I knew, he was in front of me, thanking me for waiting for him. I didn't have the heart to tell him I actually wasn't. I was waiting for the patrons to leave and clear the parking lot and get my head back on right."

"Yes, Mr. Falcon did mention you seemed just a tad out of it, but also attributed it to the wine, although he wondered if it might have been drugged. He was having Lt. Osnike, the fire investigator, look into it, along with the state lab. They found Xanax in your blood stream. Do you normally take Xanax?"

"No. I'm not on any medication. Why do you think Skye set the fires?"

"He had opportunity. He had the makings of the fire bombs in his house and garage."

"The basement?"

"Yes. Why? What do you know about what was in the basement?"

"When he brought me to stay with him after my house fire, he asked I not go down into the basement. He said it was a mess and he was concerned for my safety."

"Did he know where you lived?"

"Not exactly. He could have overheard when I was telling you. Or when I used the phone that night at his friend's place to contact some the credit card companies and make sure they were canceled, as well as my cell phone service."

"Was there any time you were apart while at

his friend's place?"

"Yes. I retired to a bedroom upstairs. He said he was going to sleep on the couch downstairs to make sure it was safe. He had all night where he wasn't in my sight."

"Did he know where your car was?"

"Yes. We were planning on going to the impound lot to pick it up later on Saturday, but then when we were at the station talking to Lt. Osnike, the call came in and I heard the address of my house for the fire. Skye drove me there, following the trucks."

"How was he acting when the call came in, or as you drove over there? How was he acting when you arrived at the scene?"

"Worried. He knew I had Tinkerbell here, in the house, and I was concerned for her. Scared, even."

"Isn't it true he ran into the house to save the cat?"

"Yes. He got some gear from the back of his truck, put it on and went in to look for her. I told him she hides in closets when she is scared, so he was checking them."

"He got gear from the back of his truck?"

"Yes."

"He found the cat?"

"Yes."

"So, essentially, he saved the day? He was a hero to you?"

She paused, frowning. "Yes. I guess so. I was very grateful he saved Tinkerbell."

"Why didn't you go to the impound lot to get your car later that day?"

"He thought it best to leave it where it was at, just in case the arsonist used it to track me. He had already destroyed the club, my house, and tried to run me down. He said you also recommended not to go to the impound lot just yet."

"So, essentially, Mr. Falcon made sure you had no transportation outside of him driving you everywhere?"

She didn't like where this was going. With the club burning, he protected her. Then he saved her cat, brought her to his home, took her to see the damaged done to her car after it blew up in the impound lot, drove her everywhere. He had become her protector, caring for her and making sure she was safe. These questions, however, sent her down a different line of thought.

"I guess."

"Did you see Mr. Falcon use his own cell phone during any of these events just prior to the fires?"

"Well, no, not exactly."

"Can you elaborate, please?"

"Well, when the club went up, he was driving to get away from the car that was chasing us. However, before my house went up, he used his phone at the station, though I'm not sure what for, and then he was using his phone to talk to people before the call came in about my car at the lot. What was in the basement? What did you find in the house?"

"The chemicals the state lab found in the club fire, and again at your house, were found in his basement on a work table. There were also several phone parts along with those chemicals."

"Phone parts?"

"We have determined cell phones were used to detonate the bombs. We are unsure if they were set as a timer or if someone called in to set them off."

"Oh my god! This can't be happening! Are you telling me there is evidence that he is the arsonist? That he started all those fires? That I was trusting my life to him and he has been trying to kill me?"

"Yes to everything except the last part. We don't think he was trying to kill you. Most arsonists enjoy the fire, the power it gives them. It is very rare they turn from starting fires to killing people, unless there is some type of catalyst. And if he really wanted you dead, he didn't have to save your life."

"Why? What would he have to gain by setting those fires?"

"If, as we suspect, he is the arsonist, he could just be a psychopath. He enjoys the role of being a hero. The attention it gives him. The power to start something so destructive and know that it was by his hand. We are still trying to figure out motive, but your answers have helped greatly."

"What do I do now?"

"I can have an officer take you to a hotel or something. You can't go back to his place, as it is the scene of an investigation. Or, if you are so inclined, Mr. Falcon used his one phone call to speak to a Raul Montego. Mr. Montego can take you someplace as well."

"Is Raul here?"

"If he isn't at the moment, I doubt if he would be much longer. He was on his way the last I heard."

"And what about Skye? Will you be releasing him, as well?"

"No. At this time he is under arrest and will spend a few nights in jail."

"I can't believe this is happening. I am just so astounded."

"Come on. I'll walk you out into the lobby where you can wait for Mr. Montego." Although

Raul set her nerves on edge, she was desperate. Like an automaton, she walked through the station to meet with Raul.

Chapter Seventeen

Raul met Kendall at the station. After talking for a few minutes and exchanging pure disbelief Skye was the arsonist, Raul convinced her to stay with him until things straightened out.

Pulling into his garage, he shut the door and told her to go inside. She could borrow the same room she stayed in the last time she was there. While Kendall went inside and headed up to the room with Tinkerbell in her carrier, Raul closed the door before he headed inside and got himself a beer. As he leaned against the kitchen sink, his eyes kept traveling over to the staircase, listening for any sounds she made as she moved about the room.

Kendall wasn't ugly. A little fuller in the body than he preferred most of his women, but then it really didn't matter when it came to getting off. He debated for a bit longer, then reached in the cupboard, pulled out a wine glass and filled it halfway with brandy. He then reached in again and took out a small bottle. Grabbing his beer and her glass, he headed upstairs and knocked lightly on her door.

He could hear her footsteps as she approached. He was almost surprised to see her eyes red, her cheeks flushed from crying. He held out the brandy. "I thought you might like something with a bit of a bite to settle your nerves. I'm sure this evening has been trying."

Kendall took the glass gratefully. Taking a sip, she coughed slightly as the alcohol burned the back of her throat. She was surprised at how warm it instantly made her insides. "Thank you. It has been a hectic and difficult day. I still can't believe any of this is happening."

"Do you want company?"

"I appreciate the thought, Raul, but I think I am just going to enjoy this and try to get some rest. I have a feeling it's going to be a long day tomorrow, and I am going to need to figure some stuff out. I wouldn't be very good company."

"I understand. I'll leave you to it, then. If you need me or anything, just call."

"Thanks again. For everything. I can't tell you how grateful I am. I owe you big time."

"Don't worry about it, Kendall." Then added silently, *You'll pay me back with interest soon enough.*

He shut the door and headed down the hall to his room. He wanted to prepare a couple of things first and give her a chance to finish the brandy before he visited her again.

Once the door was shut, Kendall moved back towards the bed, setting the brandy on the nightstand beside it. She was such a fool. She had begun to really care for Skye and look how that turned out? She thought maybe the fates, or even the spiritual guidance of her mother, was causing her to be continuously pushed into Skye's company. Shit. She couldn't have been more wrong. *He* was causing the fires. *He* was arranging it for her to be in trouble so he could be the hero and save her. It was just a game to him. A game of a warped psychopath who found her vulnerable. He must have been laughing the whole time. How could he be so cruel? How could anyone be so heartless and cold? But then, that was the clinical description of a psychopath. She started to reach for the glass again, but Tinkerbell had another idea. Jumping, she caused the glass to tip off the nightstand. Kendall jumped up, shooed Tinkerbell away in utter disgust, and went to get some tissues or a towel to clean up the spill before it stained. Raul had been kind enough to let her stay here without her ruining his stuff.

"Bad Tinkerbell. Bad," she said, though she really couldn't be very angry at her furry companion. Tinkerbell has been through so much herself the past few days, and one thing about most cats, they didn't like leaving the safety of their home, even when there was no home left. So much loss. Everything gone. Kendall stopped scrubbing the stain, overcome by a sense of grief mixed with a profound loneliness. For just a brief, silly, school-girl moment, she thought Skye was being so nice to her because he liked her. Instead he only used her for an alibi or something. Tinkerbell moved over to her, placing her paw on Kendall's thigh and giving a soft mew. She scooped the cat into her arms and buried her face into Tinkerbell's soft fur. Why was she still here? On this Earth? There was nothing left for her but her imagination and books and dreams of things she wished desperately for but could never have. After a few more moments of self pity, she set Tinkerbell aside and finished cleaning up. Once accomplished, she moved the empty glass to the bathroom counter, and then got ready for bed.

Raul had kept his door open. He noticed when she used the restroom in the hallway before returning to the bedroom. He watched the light under Kendall's door diligently, listened as she moved about, and was keenly aware when the lights went out. Another few minutes. That was all he needed; his excitement was already growing.

Chapter Eighteen

The black Corvette with the darkened windows was parked far enough away no one would have paid any attention to it, and yet close enough he could watch everything that went on at the house where Kendall was. How fortuitous the male who picked her up from the police station was his main reason for coming to this town? If only she hadn't possibly seen him, things would have been so much easier.

There was a part of him that enjoyed the destruction the fire created as it burned bright. The blue and orange of the flames as they danced towards the sky and greedily consumed everything in their wake. The flame was a hunger that couldn't and wouldn't be sated, spreading to encompass the entirety of the offering served to it in sacrifice. A consecration proposed by him to sanctify the atrocities that have occurred and cleanse it of the hideous acts that needed to be purified—something only obtained by the beautiful tongues of the fire.

Zebart sat back in the seat, pondering what he was going to do next. He wasn't a killer, not really. Circumstances changed, and in order to complete his work he would need to take care of possible loose ends. She was a loose end. She could ruin everything if he didn't stop her. However, he was determined to kill Raul, and that had been his secondary purpose when he accepted his mission. However, Kendall he felt a bit guilty about.

He failed at the club, trying to run her down. He had hoped the drink he slipped her would have slowed her down enough to complete his attempt, but he hadn't counted on the dancer who also seemed to be part of the fire department. He had a goal, and nothing or no one, not even Kendall Roberts, was going to stop him. Yet, instead, she led him to the home of the male he was anxious to beat to death. Two birds. One stone. He couldn't have asked for anything better.

He reached up to his visor and pulled down the photo he had clipped there. The woman in the photo was young, beautiful and full of life. His daughter, Zerena. Everything fell apart when she was killed. His wife had already been gone for three years prior, so it was just him and his daughter. But after her death, his place of business, his entire belief system, just fell to the wayside. She embodied his goodness. She embodied his entire world, and with her gone, nothing mattered anymore.

Zebart could still see her as she was in the morgue when he had to identify the body. Bruised, broken. Marks around her throat showing she had been strangled. Black eye and cuts on the side of her face indicated she had been beaten. Bruises on her knuckles and defensive wounds on her arms and legs inferred she had put up a fight. Still, it wasn't enough to save her, only acknowledge the horrific moments before her death.

Raped, tortured and killed. Even death couldn't bring peacefulness to her, as it should have, because of what she endured just prior to those final moments of life. Was she aware of what was about to befall her? Did she know her time on this Earth was about to be over? Was fear her only last thought, or did she think of her family? Did she cry out for her father, only to be ignored? Did she plead for mercy, only to have it rejected?

Regardless, he hadn't been there to save his daughter, his only child. He had not been around to even notice the trouble she had garnered for herself. He should have known she needed money. He should've known she was having financial difficulties. And he should've been more willing to give her anything she needed. Now, he couldn't. Any chance he had was stolen from him by the man who murdered her. But, he could correct that mistake. Zebart would make Raul pay for what he took.

Zebart got out of the Corvette, and with a swiftness belying his age, he ran down the half block to the house. Checking around to make sure he wasn't noticed, he headed to the back and began stealthily looking for a way inside.

Chapter Nineteen

Raul entered Kendall's room. The cat ran out past him and down the stairs. He didn't care. He killed a human, about to do it again, what did it matter about a cat he would eliminate when he was done having fun? Not a blessed thing. He didn't bother closing the door behind him as he walked across the darkened room, his eyes adjusting to the gloom without any problem thanks to the illumination from the hallway.

He threw her covers back and was on top of her just as Kendall's eyes flew open. She tried to scream, but his hand over her mouth prevented it. She struggled under him, but became still as he leaned his mouth against her ear. "It's okay, Kendall. This will be fun. You will see. You will enjoy it. Relax and have fun."

It was almost a soft command and she thought he had gone crazy. Did he really expect her to just lay there and enjoy sex with him? What had she done that gave him any indication she was interested in him to begin with? Yes, he had a very nice physique. He was handsome. The women at the club swooned for him. So why did he feel the need to force her when he could have so many willing others who would pay for the chance to be with him?

Maybe if she were calm, he would get that way, too, and she could point out the error of his ways. When he removed his hand from her mouth, she decided to ask him in an imperturbable tone, "What about Skye? He's your friend. He asked you to protect me, not hurt me."

Her question surprised him. She seemed lucid and not drugged at all. He had put ecstasy into her brandy and she should have been out, for the most part, or supple and willing at worse. Yet she fought him, tried to scream, and now was asking lucid questions. He couldn't imagine what happened to the beverage he prepared for her, but he couldn't think about that now. He would just have to change tactics.

"Skye is a fool. After a few weeks, he won't even miss you, and that is only if he is found innocent of setting those fires. Otherwise, he will be too busy not getting pumped in prison. They like pretty boys like him."

"He'll miss me."

"He will figure you just ran away."

"Let me go. I won't tell him anything. Or anyone else. This can be our secret."

"Why are you even lucid? Didn't you drink the brandy?"

"You drugged it?"

He didn't answer. Instead, he pinned her down more, using his weight and position against her. Before she had a chance, his free hand was on her panties and he ripped them off, the material tearing extremely loud to her ears. She started to struggle again, trying to buck him off of her. She realized Raul was already naked, most likely having entered her room in that condition. Her eyes darkened with her fury and he must have realized she was not being a willing recipient to his forced attentions.

She let out an ear-piercing scream. He backhanded her so hard her head snapped and she became dazed. Ringing in her head, stars actually appeared to her. She had always thought it was an exaggeration that one would see stars if hit hard enough. It wasn't. She saw them. Before she could recover, Raul hit her again. The stars became more prominent.

Suddenly, the weight on her body was gone. She could hear a thump on the floor beside her, but she was still too dazed to figure out what was going on. The next thing she knew, a cloth was pressed against her nose and mouth with a foul-smelling odor. Then everything became black.

Chapter Twenty

Kendall felt like her head was part of some construction area and a jackhammer was desperately trying to crack into her inner skull. Her eyes felt almost glued shut and she felt a bit nauseous. She could hear someone moving around as toxic, foul odors permeated the air. She felt danger, but not from Raul. This was something different and more sinister.

She wondered if she should try to move and figure out a way to escape or recoup for a few more minutes while she tried to decipher what was going on around her. The remaining still won out, if for nothing but the sake of her pounding, throbbing head.

She felt a presence beside her; still, she didn't move.

"I know you are awake, Kendall. Your breathing changed. It's funny, you know. Something so subtle can indicate so many things."

Realizing her ruse was discovered, she worked on opening up her eyes and ended up staring into a face that was familiar and yet, not.

"I'm sorry for this, Kendall. When you next see my daughter, tell her I'm sorry I wasn't there for her, but I am making up for it."

"Your daughter?" And then it hit her like a ton of bricks falling on her already-pulsating head. "Mr. Holiday?" Although the tone was questioning, she knew for a fact who it was. The last time she had seen him, he had been a shell of the man whom she had met once prior to her friend's funeral.

Zerena was one of her best friends. College roommates who stayed in touch after. The first time she met Mr. Holiday, she was giving Zerena a lift back to school after summer break in their senior year. Kendall owned an old pickup truck back then and it was perfect for moving students in and out of their dorms. Zerena had been Kendall's roommate the previous year and they just became so close, they put down each other to room together for their last year at school.

Kendall had pulled up to Zerena's home. Once the truck was in park, she headed up the walkway but hadn't reached the door when Zerena came running out to greet her with a huge hug. Zerena's father was on her heel and carrying a few boxes, which he loaded into the truck for his daughter. Zerena introduced them both before she ran back inside to get her suitcases.

It was while Zerena was back in the house that Mr. Holiday stopped Kendall, thrusting a hundred dollars into her hand.

"What's this for?" she asked, totally surprised looking at the money held within her palm.

"Use it for gas to get to school. Have dinner on me, whatever. I appreciate you coming to pick her up, and I know she won't have the finances or the forethought to offer you anything for the ride."

"She didn't have to, sir. She is my friend and my roommate, and I was glad to swing by and get her and her effects."

"All the same, I know how rough college can be financially. Having a little bit of money to help with gas and a decent dinner after the hard work of moving in is the least I can do."

She thanked him profusely. The money really did help with the cost of gas, and even bought a decent Chinese dinner to enjoy as they unpacked into the room for the year. He had been so kind and one could tell instantly how much he loved his daughter, as well as how proud he was of her.

The second time she met him was just heartbreaking. It was the first time she ever saw anyone so distraught, full of despair and despondent. He was a broken man. When she entered the funeral home, he hadn't even recognized her or how she knew his daughter. Every time she tried to explain, he would stare at Zerena in the coffin, as if he couldn't believe she was really just lying there. The morticians had done a very good job in preparing her, for the bruises and cuts she had been warned about were minimally visible.

Kendall, herself, couldn't believe it was real. Zerena was gone. No more getting together for an all night movie-athon, or talking on the phone for hours about everything under the sun. Her school friend was gone. Zerena and Kendall shared everything. Kendall didn't know Zerena when her mother died, and Zerena was gone by the time Kendall's mom grew sick and passed. Kendall hadn't understood the agony Zebart was suffering. She didn't have the personal experience of losing first a life partner and then a child, but she recognized his grief with one of her own.

Now, Zebart nodded in acknowledgement of who he was as he stood back from Kendall's form.

"Mr. Holiday, what is going on? Why am I tied up? Why are you here? I don't understand."

"I know, my dear child. I know. I am sorry you are caught up in this. You are a good friend to Zerena, but I have to wonder if you know. Do you know? Do you know what she does to earn money?"

Kendall recognized the fact he was still talking about his daughter in the present tense, as if she were still alive. She wasn't sure, however, if it was on purpose, or if he was just so far in denial that he didn't realize it. Zerena had confided in Kendall that she danced at a strip club. Although she had earned a college degree, she couldn't find a job that paid anything more than minimum wage and her student loans wouldn't leave her any living expense money. Dancing allowed her to pay her loans back and still have money for rent, food, gas and anything else she wanted.

"Yes. I knew she danced."

"Danced? She took her clothes off in front of men for money."

"She didn't have a choice, Mr. Holiday. Not everyone can get a fantastic-paying job as a chemist coming out of the gate. Although she was good, her grade point average was a 4.2. In today's competitive world, chemists weren't being hired without experience or a 4.7. No one would hire her to give her experience with money enough to pay off her loans. She did the best she could, and it was only supposed to be temporary until she earned enough to get in the black."

"You know she was killed by a fucking john?

Some guy she hooked up with at the club bought her and used her, then killed my baby?" His voice cracked at the end of the sentence. She could still see the pain on his face, hear it in his words and her heart broke for him. Just for those brief few moments, she felt for him. Losing his family had to have been devastating. Hell, it was for her.

"I heard at the funeral, but they didn't know who it was."

"I know. It's him." He moved to the side so she could see beyond him. Seated in another chair and tied up was Raul. He was still unconscious, with a thick streak of blood streaming down the side of his face, but thankfully wearing a pair of boxers.

"Is he alive?"

"For the moment. He is going to slowly pay for what he did to my daughter. What he tried to do to you."

Clarity of his words made her remember a nude Raul on top of her, ripping her panties away as he tried to force himself on her. She looked down at herself. She was still wearing the t-shirt she had found the last time she was there. Oversized, it covered enough of her. She closed her eyes for a moment as dawning realization dripped over her like molasses. When she reopened them again, she turned back to Zebart. "How do you know? If you have evidence, why not turn it over to the police?"

"Because they won't do anything. The police will arrest him, question him and, at best, throw him in jail where the taxpayers will pay for him to eat, sleep and watch television. He needs to pay for what he did! He needs to pay!"

"Okay. I can understand that. How do you know for sure it was him?" Granted, she wasn't forgetting about her own experience or the creepy, cold feeling overcoming her whenever he was nearby. She assumed Raul's manhandling was why her head throbbed as badly as it currently did.

Zebart had been fiddling around with what she could only assume was a bomb on the table. With her question, he finished up securing the cell phone with duct tape to what looked like sparklers and plastic containers filled with various colored liquids, all sitting in some kind of a plastic bowl with some silver and black dust at the bottom. Standing, he began to pace slightly, glancing at Raul, waiting for him to awaken.

"I didn't plan to be the proverbial villain and lay forth all my dastardly deeds like some B-rated movie, but I want him to know why and how he is going to die. I want him aware of what is happening to him. So, I need him to wake up first. Out of respect for you, I will elaborate how I know it was this scum.

"Zerena left an Instagram of herself. It wasn't uncovered until months later when I was going through her things. She had labeled it wrong, or sent it to the wrong address, or however that shit works. Anyways, it was stuck in limbo for a long while after the police released all her things out of evidence, not having found anything. Stupid fucks. They're supposed to have experts to figure this shit out and me, who is only slightly computer literate, enough to do what I need it to do, eventually figured out her Instagram account and saw the video. In it, she talks about meeting a male dancer named Raul and how excited she was they were going to get together. Compare moves or some such shit. In the video, there was a brief picture of him at the bar getting drinks. I had checked out several other male dance clubs and coed dance clubs, but none contained a Raul. At least not one who wasn't gay, and none that looked like him.

"When I saw him a few nights back at that strip club you were at, I realized it was him. I thought about calling the police, but I just couldn't bring myself to do it. He was mine. I was going to make him pay for what he did to my baby."

"And me? Why are you trying to kill me? I didn't hurt Zerena. She was my best friend."

"I know. You were hers, too. However, I couldn't leave loose ends. I still have more work to accomplish, and if you told them it was me, then my work would end."

"I'm a loose end? How am I a loose end? What kind of work? I don't understand any of this."

Zebart stopped and stared at her. "You didn't

see me at the club?"

"Not that I am aware of. I was really zoned out for the most part. What I did notice was the groups of women going in and not wanting to look like I was alone."

"You didn't see the beer truck or me unloading?"

"I vaguely remember a truck pulling in, but other than that, no."

"Then I am really sorry, Kendall. I really am. I was sure you saw me. If you told them about me, then I couldn't continue burning the clubs down, putting them out of business and saving all those daughters, unlike I was able to save mine. Maybe, if she didn't have the club to go to, my baby wouldn't have met Raul and she would still be alive. I figured you saw me, recognized me and would tell the police who was setting the fires. I couldn't risk that.

"I tried to make your death quick and easy. I gave you a drink with my Xanax in it to calm you down and slow your reflexes. I didn't know you would be followed out of the bar or had your own protector. Everything just got strange then. I didn't know where you disappeared to, or how to find you. Setting your house on fire brought you back out, but then I lost you again. Blowing up the car got you out again, and this time I followed you to your rescuer's home. I was then able to keep tabs on where you were. I couldn't believe my luck when Raul came and got you from the police station. Two birds. One stone. Perfect. I am sorry, though. You were good to my daughter, so you understand I have to do this for her."

"Mr. Holiday. Please. I won't tell anyone. Just let me go. If for nothing else, for Zerena. She would be unhappy if you hurt her best friend."

"Maybe, but it's too late. I can't take the chance. I have too much work yet to do and I can't be stopped. I can't take the chance."

"I swear. Please. Let me go."

"Sorry. I really am."

Raul groaned as he started to come to, turning both Kendall's and Zebart's attention towards him. Kendall was still furious at what he tried to do to her. As a result, she was grateful for Zebart's interference, saving her from rape and possibly worse. If, in fact, as Zebart had revealed to her just minutes ago, Raul had killed Zerena, she could very well have been next on his list. Of course, dying *with* Raul wasn't any better, other than she avoided the sexual assault.

Think, Kendall. Think. There has to be a way out of this.

Chapter Twenty-One

"I didn't do it. I'm not the arsonist. Come on, Barney. You have known me for years. How can you even think it's me?" Skye was frustrated and annoyed over this whole thing. If it wasn't for the fact he knew Kendall was safe with Raul, he would really be freaking out. He didn't know why, but he just felt she was better protected with him around. Being detained in an interrogation room or a holding cell was not productive to appeasing his anxiety.

"There are too many coincidences, such as the items found in your home or the fact every place Kendall was suddenly exploded. The club, her house, her car, all engulfed in flames. Add to that your parents dying in a fire of unknown causes…"

"Are you fucking kidding me with this? My parents were years ago."

"True. It just looks suspicious. Then and now. You gained quite a substantial sum with their deaths. Enough you don't need to work ever, yet you do. You have motive, means, and opportunity by using remote triggers. Your fixation on Ms. Roberts is puzzling, but the rest?"

Skye ran a hand through his hair. "Okay. I will admit it looks awfully strange and there are a lot of coincidences here. But if I told you once, I've told you a thousand times: I didn't set those fires. The chemicals and phones in the basement are just experiments. I'm trying to get them working, and if I do, I donate them to our men overseas. Check with the American Legion. I've already got over a dozen working and turned them over to be shipped. The stuff in the garage were my parents' things that I just never disposed of. And my parents dying in the fire doesn't even deserve acknowledgement for such a ludicrous theory. Especially when it had been put to bed ages ago."

"Look, Skye. What do you want me to do here? A partial had been found on a timer, a burner used to set off the fire at the club. A partial that you can fit. You had the opportunity, you had the materials."

"I don't have motive."

"Psychopaths don't necessarily need one."

"God damn it, Barney. Do you think I am a cold-hearted and calculating bastard?"

"I honestly don't know what to think here." Barney was interrupted for anything further when a knock at the door disturbed them. The door cracked open enough for a female in a police uniform to poke her head in. "Sir? Officer Charles and Lt. Commander Melancroft would like to see you a moment."

Without an additional word, Barney stood, scooping up the file he had lying on the table in front of him and departed the room, shutting the door behind him. Skye was left alone, again. If he could, he would walk out and find Kendall. Surprisingly, it was this time away from her that his concern for her grew and he realized he needed her in his life. He wanted her in his life. She was everything he desired: strong, intelligent, kind, warm and, most importantly to him, she saw him as a person, not a piece of meat. He was even given some hope before the police arrived. She was interested in men, not women, and that just made his day. He had a chance to woo her to him, and once he got out of here, he planned on doing just that.

Somehow, someway, he was going to make her want him as much as he wanted her. First, he needed to get out of here. He didn't know why, exactly, but he was anxious. It was as if he sensed she was in trouble, despite the fact he knew she was safe with Raul. So why this feeling of impending doom?

Barney headed down the hall to the office of Lt. Commander Melancroft.

"Come in, come in." Brandon Melancroft waved Barney in when he saw him. "Have a seat."

Brett Charles nodded towards Barney, then passed him a report. He didn't look none-to-happy as he did so. Barney took the papers and scanned through them, his own frown increasing.

"As you can see, Barn, looks like you might have the wrong guy."

"Has anyone checked Skye's alibi for all these occurrences?"

"Yeah. You think we'd bother your interrogation if we hadn't? We talked to Michael Walso, the owner of the club. Every single one of those fires occurred when he was performing or too far away for him to get to from the time he was finished. Even with remote controls, they would have to have been planted in a reasonable amount of time so as not to have been discovered prior to their being set off. Mr. Falcon just didn't have the time to accomplish this, from what we can ascertain.

"Mr. Walso even sent over video surveillance that showed Mr. Falcon either still at the club working or having just left. As much as I wish to say it was him, he just couldn't have gone there and gotten back in time. Some of the areas are over a ten-hour drive from here. He is not our guy."

"So we have a serial arsonist who is… What? Burning down strip clubs around the state and across the borders?"

"Pretty much. And here is something else. Until

the other night, all the strip clubs were gentlemen clubs. Girl dancers. Cock-a-doodle was the first male club hit. Ms. Roberts' home—the first personal property we have detected, though we could just be unaware of others. Ms. Roberts' car is also the first vehicle we are aware of by the same person. But again, it could just be they were never connected before now. I have to wonder why the MO has changed once Ms. Roberts came into the picture. So far, we cannot find any connection to his obsession with her."

Barney tossed the report onto the lieutenant's desk. "I'm glad Skye is innocent. I hated thinking one of my guys, especially a POC, was involved."

"You want to give him the good news that he is free to go?" Brandon asked.

"Yeah. I'll take care of it. Thanks." Barney shook both men's hands then left the office to return to the interrogation room where Skye was sitting just as he left him minutes before.

"Good news, at least for you."

"You found the guy and realized it wasn't me?"

"Something like that. We found he has set several other fires at clubs throughout the state, as well as in neighboring states. Mike Walso confirmed you couldn't have done them, as did some surveillance tapes he had."

Skye looked at him. He had been preparing himself for the worst even though he knew he was innocent. Still, it surprised him to be released so quickly. He figured he would've had at least a couple of nights in jail before they discovered he wasn't behind the fires.

"Come on, Skye. I'll drive you home."

"No." Barney's words broke the stunned spell he had been under. "No. Can you take me to Raul's?"

"You really like her?"

"Yeah. I do."

"I always thought of you more with someone like Monique or Debra."

"Those two are more interested in themselves and what they can get from guys than anything important or real. Kendall is special."

"Glad someone caught your interest, but you need to be careful. Someone is still trying to kill her. For whatever reason we have yet to discern. Anyone caught with her could be collateral damage."

"Or, it could make the difference in saving her life. Like pushing her outta the way of a car planning on gunning her down. I'll take my chances."

"Alright. Let's get your stuff and I'll get you to Raul's. Can you get home from there? You might want to wait until morning, though. I think the police are still finishing up and leaving. You might not want to see it until after a good night's rest."

"That will be up to Raul, but I have no problems with that condition. Can we just go now?"

"Of course. Come on."

Barney led him to the holding area where they retrieved Skye's personal belongings, which had been removed upon his arrest. Once all the papers were signed and everything was in order, they headed out to Barney's department vehicle and headed to Raul's home, guided by Skye's directions.

As they turned down the street of Raul's house, Skye saw something that made his blood turn ice cold. "That's the car. Fuck! Barney! That's the car that tried to run down Kendall."

"Are you sure?"

"Corvette. Blackened windows, smudged license. I swear that's the car. Hard to forget a vehicle aiming to kill you."

Barney got on the radio to call it in as he pulled past Raul's house before stopping. Without waiting for backup or anything else, Skye was out of the truck and stealthily made his way over, checking the house. When he noticed a broken hinge on the back door, he alerted Barney, who was watching but still staying back. Barney nodded in acknowledgement and called in additional information over the department frequency.

Skye wasn't sure what to expect, but he knew it wasn't going to be good. Trying to keep his presence on the down low, he made his way through the house towards the lights of the kitchen. Keeping to the shadows, he heard some conversation.

It was only as he peeked around the corner that he got the lay of the land and it infuriated him to no end. He could see Raul on the far side of the kitchen, tied to a chair as he was being beaten by a man whom Skye didn't recognize. Kendall was closest to him, also confined by ropes to a chair. He could see her profile. Her porcelain skin red and swollen. Tinkerbell had jumped on her lap, probably for comfort for what was going on. On the table between Raul and Kendall was a small cell phone duct taped to some sort of crudely formed homemade bomb.

Skye had to get Kendall and Raul out of there. Her attention was on the male and Raul so she hadn't noticed him trying to get her attention. When Skye heard the distinct sound of knuckles against skin, he turned towards Raul and the man who was giving him a thorough pounding. He should run in and tackle the male, stop him from beating up his friend. But his concern was more for Kendall. He had to get her out of here. Assessing the situation and how best to proceed, he jumped back into the shadows as Raul's chair fell backwards.

A sound of wood cracking and Raul was free. He was avoiding the blows the older man was throwing. With the two of them occupied and Raul managing on his own, Skye felt better about setting his concentration on getting Kendall out. He knew Barney had called for backup, so he was more than willing to let the police deal with whatever was going on between the two of them. Raul was younger and more physically buff, so he should be able to hold his own, despite the head injury and physical, pugilistic endeavors he had been subjected to.

Keeping low, Skye got to Kendall's chair. Tinkerbell was still on her lap, and he was grateful the cat didn't startle enough to run. Pulling out a pocket knife from his back pocket, Skye proceeded to cut the ties securing her wrists behind the chair.

Kendall almost jumped when she saw Skye sneak behind her to cut her loose. She knew she needed to keep her eyes away from Skye so Zebart wouldn't catch on to his presence. Hopefully, Raul and Zebart would be too busy with each other to notice someone else in the room. Skye cut her loose and, in one swift movement, she had Tinkerbell in her arms while Skye cut the ties around her ankles. Once she was totally free, Skye grabbed her arm and quickly led her out of the house with only a glance back at the two men embroiled in a bitter battle of fisticuffs.

As soon as he got Kendall safely to Barney, he would return to assist Raul with who must surely be the arsonist and attempted murderer. He truly had no clue what was going on, but Kendall didn't seem concerned about getting out of there as quickly as possible, and he was more than willing to oblige.

Skye was concerned about Kendall. Her face was quickly becoming swollen and she seemed to have a slight bit of difficulty with her equilibrium. He would kill the man who beat her up, or help Raul do it.

Once they managed to get outside, Skye rushed

Kendall to Barney, who was waiting. He was about to go back in when Kendall stopped him. "Don't."

"Raul is in there. He needs my help."

"Raul is not who you think he is. He did this to my face."

Skye looked at her as if she just grew a second head or sprouted horns. "Why?"

"He tried to drug and rape me." She tilted her head back, pushing her hair out of the way. "I feel like my neck is bruised. If it is, he did that as well. He tried to strangle me."

"I don't understand." Skye clenched his hands into fists at his side. If any part of what she said was true, he was about to kill Raul himself. "Who is the other guy, then?"

"Mr. Holiday. He was the father to one of my best friends from college. His daughter, Zerena, was raped and murdered a few years back. He was devastated. Before Raul awoke, he told me he had evidence Raul sexually assaulted and killed her." Kendall cuddled Tinkerbell closer, the pain of what her friend must have gone through and her own loss still touched something deep within her.

"Why was he trying to kill you, then?"

Before she had a chance to answer, several police cars arrived on the scene, as did a couple of fire trucks and the paramedic units. They hadn't even gotten out of their vehicles, yet, when an explosion occurred. The detonation caused the windows to shatter outward from the house. Skye instinctively moved to block Kendall from the blast, protecting her with his own body.

Barney ducked down behind his open truck door. Spinning quickly when the initial blast discharged, Skye could see the area of the kitchen, where he earlier noticed the bomb on the table, was engulfed in flames. The firefighters ran to try and put the fire out, but Skye and Barney had seen enough destruction in the past; they were pretty sure neither Holiday nor Raul survived. And if by some mi`racle they did, they would suffer from third degree burns.

Barney informed the firemen of the two men still inside of the house, then went to speak to the officers that were there. Chaos erupted around Kendall. The firemen rushed to put out the fire and see about getting the two men out. The police were cordoning off the street so the firefighters could work without worrying about civilians interfering. Men were running in one direction while others were running in another. Pedestrians started to come out of their homes and vehicles to watch the action occurring around them.

Skye calmly but hastily walked Kendall around to the rear of an ambulance, which had just pulled up. There was a part of him that wanted to help put the fire out and see if the two men were still able to be saved, but after what he learned, he was more concerned about Kendall's wellbeing. He talked briefly to the EMTs, bringing them up to speed as to the possible extent of Kendall's injuries. They checked her out, despite her protests and extreme vocal refusal to be taken to a hospital.

Leaving Kendall temporarily, Skye headed towards the other men. He didn't have his truck with him or his turnout gear, which referred to the time saving practice of turning the pants out over the top of the boots. He made sure he stayed out of the way as he watched and waited to see what would occur next. He was almost surprised when some of the men came out of the house carrying two bodies and putting them on the awaiting gurneys to get them away from the burning abode faster.

Both men were badly burned from what Skye could see, but was unable from his vantage point to know whether or not they were still alive. He knew there was more to Kendall's story about everything that occurred this evening, including the discovery of why Raul attacked her and her friend years ago, or why Holiday tried to kill her several times the past few days. He hoped one or both of the men were still alive to tell their version of the tale.

Chapter Twenty-Two

It was hours later before the MVFD was able to get the flames under control. Kendall had been checked out and, despite their heavy recommendations to the contrary, released. She hadn't let Tinkerbell go, but then she also didn't have a safe place for her, yet, either, since the carrier was burning along with the rest of Raul's place.

Through it all, Kendall couldn't believe Raul and Mr. Holiday were dead, the latter caught in his own bomb of destruction. Somehow, the cell phone timer must have been set and gone off, or the bomb was knocked over and sparked, which started the chain reaction leading to the explosion. Regardless, they were both killed in the initial blast. Neither had a chance. After the two men had been brought out, the paramedics checked both of them out, declaring them DOA before sending them to the morgue.

While Kendall was being thoroughly examined,

Skye headed over to the Corvette, which was being probed for every minute detail. He remained far enough away so as not to interfere, yet close enough to observe everything discovered. The vehicle held a wealth of information and evidence, solidifying his innocence and further condemning Raul for his own indiscretions.

Zebart had gathered a strong case of evidence against Raul, including pictures he previously mentioned to Kendall on Zerena's Instagram. Several other details could possibly close some cold cases as a result from more evidence found against Raul for similar MOs throughout the area, including one from just a couple of weeks ago. It appears Raul had a predilection towards raping females, then strangling them to death in the throes of his own orgasm. Kendall was extremely fortunate to have been saved from such a demise.

Also uncovered were receipts for items needed and left over materials utilized to make the bombs. There was also a map indicating the locations of properties already destroyed, as well as ones Zebart had planned attacking next. There were over fifty locations marked on the map.

Realizing how close he had come to losing Kendall because he literally threw her to the jackals without knowing the man he considered not only a coworker but a friend was a pariah, Skye took his anger and frustration out on Raul's mailbox. He kicked it off its post then used the leg to beat it against the ground until it was completely destroyed. Only then did he calm down enough, shoving others away who tried to get him to stop. Kendall could be dead or worse now because of him. He could have lost her, and the idea was more than he could bear.

As Kendall watched Skye take out his vexations on the mailbox, a part of her felt awful for what he was experiencing emotionally. She, herself, was feeling overwhelmed by all the events and knowledge she had gained in the past couple of hours. She experienced sadness for Mr. Holiday, even a little for Raul dying in the explosion, yet she was mostly glad the world was free of them. The latter perception she knew was a result of them both trying to kill her. She understood Skye's way in handling the news of what Raul really was: a rapist and murderer. She wanted to beat some inanimate object, too. Raul killed her friend after taking advantage of her. The horror Zerena must have felt, gone through, and the terror she endured in her last moments had haunted her since she learned of her friend's demise. But knowing she was so close to experiencing the same thing was incomprehensible.

A part of her could understand what Mr. Holiday had been feeling: the need to kill Raul himself. He certainly achieved his wish, though she doubted he planned to also perish. From what he told her, she had the distinct feeling he was going to continue setting fires, especially to strip clubs. She assumed because he couldn't save his own daughter from such a life, he would save others by eliminating their places of business. What he hadn't considered was the dancers would just go elsewhere or fully enter prostitution.

Barney finally finished up what he needed to,

then drove Skye, Kendall and Tinkerbell to Skye's place. The crime scene tape had been removed. With the bomb and Kendall's testimony, they knew for sure Skye was innocent, just in case there were any remaining doubts.

Personally, Skye was glad to be back home and put the whole thing behind him. The last week had been wearisome, but the last 24 hours were outlandishly preposterous. At least to him. He was just glad it was all over and Kendall was truly safe. However, a part of him was also grievously disheartened as well. With her no longer needing protection from someone trying to murder her, there was no reason for her to stay. Skye wasn't quite ready to let her leave. Not yet. Not ever. Would she give him a chance?

Kendall set Tinkerbell down once they were securely inside. The feline didn't leave her side, following her like a shadow wherever she went. As did Skye, who followed on her very footsteps as she headed to the kitchen. She looked through the Keurig cups selection, choosing a Black Pekoe Tea and starting the machine.

"I think I am going to make some tea. Do you want me to get you anything?"

"I need a whiskey after everything tonight." Skye went to the cupboard and grabbed a bottle of Forty Creek Port Wood Reserve Whiskey and a small tumbler and poured himself a healthy triple shot. He downed it on two gulps, then refilled his glass and sat at the table watching her.

"I can't believe Raul tried to hurt you tonight. What the fuck was he thinking? Did he think I wouldn't miss you or notice you gone?"

"He said he planned on telling you I just left. That I didn't want to stay with him, so I left. He figured that would've been enough of an explanation, I guess."

"Well, he guessed wrong. I would've hunted you down. Searched everywhere for you."

"I appreciate that, but why?"

"Because, Kendall, I'm not ready to let you go. Not in a stalker, evil kind of way. Holy shit, you have had enough of that." Skye moved, leaving the glass on the table, and grabbed each of her upper arms, holding her to face him. "I care about you enough to make sure you left of your own accord and not just disappeared. I would search everywhere for you just to be sure you are okay. I wouldn't want to lose touch with you. I've grown very fond of you over the past few days."

"I've grown fond of you, too. Enough that you should know I wouldn't just leave without letting you know where I was. I would hate it if we lost touch. You have been very good to me, especially about giving me a place to stay since mine burned down. Since there is no longer a threat to my life, I will start looking tomorrow for another place."

"Kendall, I will respect whatever decision you make, but I am hoping you will stay here with me. I know you don't understand, and I suck at trying to explain this. You are the kind of woman I want in my life, and if you leave, I fear you will close the door on us."

"There, technically, isn't an us, Skye. Surely, you want your place back to yourself."

"Why? It's big, roomy, lonely. If it makes you feel better, you can, I don't know, buy the groceries or something. I would really like you to stay here instead of finding a place of your own."

Kendall frowned. She didn't want to get used to him being in her life. She didn't want to go through the eventual disappointment of his getting tired of her and leaving her. She didn't want to start letting someone in again, only to end up alone down the road. Kendall was still sure he was only interested in what he couldn't have, and once he had her he would be bored or realize she wasn't want he wanted. Worse, he might realize she was not beautiful and she would have to watch him be swayed by someone who looked just like Monique. She didn't think she could handle it or the rejection that would accompany it. She wasn't willing to open her heart again.

Skye must've sensed her change in mood, for he dropped his hands on her arms. "You are welcome to stay. I hope you do." He took his whiskey and headed out of the kitchen.

Kendall should've run while she had the strength, yet somehow, she found herself getting closer to the kitchen threshold, following Skye into the other room. It appeared as if her feet knew what they wanted before her head or heart did.

"Skye? Wait."

He set his drink down on the coffee table and turned to look at her with hope in his eyes.

"If the invitation is still open, I would like to stay. I can pay for the groceries, or half of whatever you owe, or whatever you would like."

"Groceries are fine. The house is paid for. Inheritance money. I'll take care of everything else: the utilities, taxes and such."

She suddenly felt uncomfortable. Wasn't this what he wanted? Wasn't this what he asked of her? Now it seemed more like a business proposition and she could only hope she hadn't made a mistake.

"Okay, then." She turned to leave the room again, stopping when Skye caught her hand and held it.

He stepped closer to her, stopping when they

were standing toe to toe. "I'm glad you are staying."

Chapter Twenty-Three

Kendall looked away. Skye was so handsome, so assured of his masculinity. She knew he was fully aware of the effect he had on women and used it to his advantage. Women most likely thought of him as a god on Earth. How could they not? No way was he wanting to be with her. She wasn't that pretty, and she was a little overweight. Granted, she wasn't what most would consider obese or even very fat, but she was certainly no size one or two, like the women she would imagine he would be attracted to and who would fawn for his attentions. At best, she was average. Unlike him, she never turned a head in her life.

Again she had to ask herself why he had approached her in the club. Why had he asked her to go on stage with him? Why had he asked her to wait after the show was over and then joined her? And for fuck sake, how had she ended up living alone with him in his house?

Maybe there actually were hidden cameras and

she would find herself on You Tube being made a fool of. Maybe this was nothing but a joke to him, or worse, god forbid, she was his charity case for the month. *You know, make the average and ugly feel special. Give them something besides an otherwise boring existence. Give them a thrill. Had I looked that fucking pathetic?*

All these thoughts and more ran through her mind in the span of the moment it took for him to be directly in front of her and tilting her chin up to meet those incredibly unreal turquoise eyes of his.

"Stay with me," he repeated softly. And in truth, she wasn't sure how to say no, or even if she truly wanted to.

Her breath caught in her throat, her heart raced and her palms were sweaty. All the classic signs of wanting to be with him intimately. She was under his spell, lost to everything but him and a look that threatened to sear her very soul.

The phone rang and it broke the trance she had been under. Sure, this night could be fun. After all, how many women get the chance to have sex with a man like Skye? But to do that, she would have to be naked and all her problem areas, all her flaws, would be exposed to someone who was perfectly formed.

Skye stepped back and pulled his phone out of his back pocket. He answered the call while he kept his eyes focused solely on the woman before him. As she reached the doorway of the room, she turned back and mouthed "sorry", disappearing quickly up the stairs.

"Skye here." His voice was low and husky from its usual tenor. "No, Monique, I'll not be attending." He followed Kendall to her room. He quickened his pace, making it there just as she began to close the heavy wooden barrier. He pushed his flat palm against it so she couldn't shut it. Skye moved so as to push her farther in, spin her around and then thrust her back against the door, closing it with his hand, but with him now inside. He pressed himself against her, trapping her between the door and his hard body. He whispered against her ear. "Don't shut me out. I'll just be a minute."

Monique? How can I compete with that woman? Kendall wondered. Good god. Monique was a perfect size one, long shapely legs and an hourglass figure. She had long, soft-looking, silky hair. She was certainly the perfect woman for Skye, matching him in looks. Monique was the kind of woman who turned heads, who men noticed as soon as she entered their line of vision and who vied for her attention all night long in hopes of being the one she would let in her bed by the end of the evening.

"No, Monique. I'm not interested and I'm not alone."

Kendall didn't hear him, really. Her mind was solely on escaping with some dignity intact, which was quickly becoming more problematic by the second. His breath was still against her neck, his hand played with her hair, twirling it about his finger. Skye still had her pressed against the door, preventing her escape. He whispered to her again. "I'm almost finished."

Why in the hell would he want me when Monique was calling for him? Was this a game to him? And if so, what were the rules? The objective? Kendall couldn't believe anyone would want her for herself. It just didn't make any sense.

"Gotta go. Don't call back," Skye growled into the phone, flicking it closed and tossing it onto the dresser nearby, not caring that it clattered to the floor instead. "Please, don't tell me to leave."

She managed to tilt her head up to face him, though she kept her eyes lowered. She knew they would give her away. "I didn't want to bother you. Monique…" Her voice drifted off. Kendall was nothing like Monique or the other women who appeared in pictures around his place. Again, the thought of Monique made Kendall realize how inadequate she was for Skye.

With his free hand, he tilted her chin up, searching her face and somehow gleaning all the knowledge he wanted from her with that intense gaze. Her windows to her soul told him everything she wouldn't say to him verbally. He could see her embarrassment, her shame, her fear. He knew she didn't think herself worthy enough for anyone, let alone him. He realized only something drastic would prove to her he wanted to be solely with her. He knew at Raul's flaming building he was in love with her and he didn't want her to ever be away from him.

He would show her she was beautiful, especially to him. He would prove he could love and care for her, no matter what it took. As he pulled back, he took her hand and pulled her with him. She wasn't sure where he was dragging her until he moved her in front of a tri-fold, full-length mirror, which stood by the closet of her room. Releasing her hand, he wrapped his arm around her waist to keep her planted in front of him. With his free hand he began to unbutton her blouse. Slowly, with deliberate movements, he pulled it off her.

Kendall was unsure why she was standing there letting him do this instead of running away. Maybe she was tired of running. More likely, she was curious to see what he was doing and why, unsure if it was truly occurring. Before she realized he had moved away to take the shirt off, he was behind her again, rubbing her with his body once again. His hand moved up her bare thigh, lifting her skirt as he did so. Kendall had to admit she was thoroughly entranced, unable to move or breathe despite her embarrassment. She should be screaming for him to stop touching her. She should force him to leave, but she knew he realized the truth when he gazed into her eyes. She was head over heels in love with him. At this moment, she would give him whatever he asked and pay the price later. Heaven help her, she was weak when it came to her desire for him.

Skye moved quickly and with assuredness. In minutes, she was virtually bare before him and the unforgiving mirror wearing only her bra and panties. Kendall couldn't stand to look at herself. All her flaws and imperfections glaring at her. She started to look away, but Skye gripped her chin from behind and forced her to look at their mutual reflection. Her almost-naked, imperfect body and his clothed, chic polo and jeans fitted perfectly over his sculpted body that she could only imagine was even more impressive sans clothes.

She cringed inwardly, ashamed. Maybe if she went to the gym more often or even got a gym membership. But shit, who had the time or the energy? Even her home exercise bike was used better as a clothing rack than for anything near its intended use.

"What do you see in that mirror?" Skye kept his eyes on hers through the reflection.

Kendall looked down at her feet, noticing she was still wearing her shoes but little else. "Nothing."

Skye shook his head, a single lock falling on his forehead. "No, Kendall. There is everything."

"How can you say that?" Her mind went to perfect Monique and how she failed horribly in comparison.

Skye seemed to know where her thoughts drifted as he addressed them almost immediately. "If I wanted body perfection, I'd be at Monique's side at this very moment. But where she may have what most consider the perfect body, that's all she has. Personally, I don't care for someone that thin or artificial. Kendall, when I see you, my breath catches in my throat. You're so fucking beautiful and it's made more so because of your kind heart, loving soul, and mostly because you don't even see it." Skye paused, his eyes giving her a hot look filled with so many unspoken promises. Placing his hands on her shoulders, he turned her around away from the mirror. Grabbing her hand in the process, he put it against the hard, firm bulge in his pants. His voice was thick, husky with desire as soon as her hand was against him.

"If you still want me to leave, I'll go, but I'd rather you let me stay, because I want you. I want to show you in a multitude of ways how much I desire you."

Kendall was surprised at his words. He *wanted* her? Those words spoke a volume of promises and rich desires to be fulfilled. She was totally surrendering to him, whether or not her head agreed.

"Take me." Any resolve she might have had went right out the window, along with every concern she had imagined. He wanted her. She couldn't have heard anything better, even if she tried to think of something. His words of wanting her, his hardness against her hand, his desire deep within his voice was better than anything she could dream of. It was better than winning the lottery.

Hell, it was better even than chocolate, and that alone said a great deal. Chocolate was her one true solace and treat to herself. Savoring that delectable sweetness was a comfort that never failed her. But this surpassed even chocolate.

Someone wanted her, even if it was just for one night. For this singular instance, she was someone. Not because Skye wanted her or made her feel special as a result, but because she felt someone actually perceived her. She was no longer invisible. At least with him, she made a difference in someone else's life. She made a mark and touched someone, if but for a brief moment, and it was a feeling that would last for a long time, even if she became invisible once again when this night was over. It was an experience she would know for one night.

She was made to feel special and no one could ever take that feeling away from her. Not ever.

It was then it hit her like a ton of bricks. "No. No. Wait. I can't do this." Holy shit, she was standing with the bare minimum on in front of him thinking about letting him have his one-night stand. Even going so far as to tell him to take her, like some wanton whore. Was she so far gone with the trauma of the past week and then his kind, gentle words she was willing to be so reckless?

Skye's face fell. He closed his eyes and she could see his jaw moving as he tried to regain some control. She grabbed a robe she had lying nearby and wrapped it around her body. The images of her hideousness would remain with him forever. There was no way he could un-see that.

"Can I ask why?" His voice was still low, husky and dripping with desire.

"I don't want a one-night stand. I'm not one for casual sex. I never have been."

"That's what you think I want? One night? Casual? If that were the case, I would've tried the first night you were here, but I respected you enough to get to know you and let you come to know me. If I wanted casual sex, or a few nights of shooting my load, I'd stick with someone who was artificial, like Monique. Someone who's only interested in themselves and getting off. I don't want that. I want someone who I enjoy spending time with, who is intelligent and sweet, someone who has substance. Someone, Kendall, like you.

I don't want a fling. I want to start something serious. I love the way you look at the good in people, the way you have such compassion, and the way you have a love for life. You're amazing, smart and tender. I'm not saying these things just to get in your pants. I'm saying them because this is how I actually feel. I've fallen in love with you, Kendall. If you will have me, I would like to be something more than just some casual fling. Give me a chance. I know you've been through a lot, but I want to be here for you. Please, Kendall. Give me a chance. Let me be why you'll never have to be lonely again."

She stared at him, slightly bewildered. He was almost pleading with her to give in and she was running out of excuses. He had no reason to lie to her. Shit, he could have any girl he wanted, as she pointed out to herself numerous times already. So why lie just to get her? Plus, he stayed with her throughout everything. He even saved her life and Tinkerbell's on multiple occasions. He had no reason to be deceitful.

He seemed to know she was caving in. He moved up to her and hesitantly undid the belt of her robe. He slipped it off her shoulders as he bent down to kiss the crook of her neck. He continued to kiss up to her jaw, finally reaching her lips while simultaneously pushing the robe off to pool at her feet. Her hands moved to his waist, pulling his shirt out and pulling it over his head, tossing it onto the floor along with the rest of her clothes.

He knew, then, he had won. She was giving him the chance he all but got down on his knees and begged for. He would prove himself worthy of her. Every day. She'd never have to doubt herself again, and just as importantly, she'd never again be alone or unloved.

ABOUT THE AUTHOR

Ms. Hawks has always been interested in writing in some form or other. A few years back, she was involved with and then ran a Star Trek Interactive Writing Group which was successful for a number of years. Yes, she is a trekker and proud of it.

A few years back, she received her Master's Degree in Ancient Civilizations, Native American History and United States History.

She loves to travel, especially to attend Author/Reader conventions visiting fans and meeting new ones.

She currently lives in the Chicago area with three spoiled cats.

More From Laura Hawks

http://www.amazon.com/Demons-Kiss-Demon-Saga-Trilogy-ebook/dp/B00S8SPQ78/ref=tmm_kin_swatch_0?_encoding=UTF8&qid=1462076150&sr=1-1

Flaming Retribution

http://www.amazon.com/Demons-Dream-Demon-Saga-Trilogy:ebook/dp/B00ROC6A06/ref=tmm_kin_swatch_0?_encoding=UTF8&qid=1462076150&sr=1-4

https://www.amazon.com/Demons-Web-Demon-Trilogy-Book-ebook/dp/B01F11ZEGC/ref=sr_1_1_twi_kin_1?ie=UTF8&qid=1482179912&sr=8-1&keywords=demon%27s+web+by+laura+hawks

Flaming Retribution

http://www.amazon.com/Shifters-Hope-Spirit-Walkers-Saga-ebook/dp/B00SCK2I32/ref=tmm_kin_swatch_0?_encoding=UTF8&qid=1462076129&sr=1-2

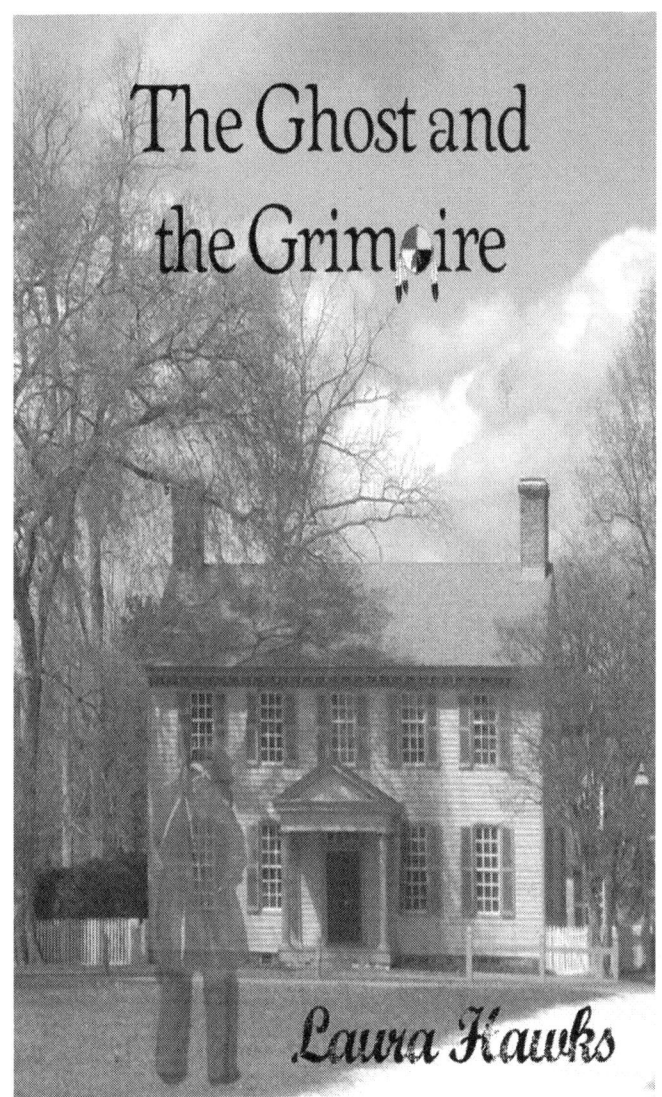

Laura Hawks

The Ghost and the Grimoire

Laura Hawks

http://www.amazon.com/Ghost-Grimoire-Laura-Hawks-ebook/dp/B017OJ18JQ/ref=tmm_kin_swatch_0?_encoding=UTF8&qid=1461904697&sr=1-3

Flaming Retribution

Made in the USA
Columbia, SC
11 February 2021